SHARON RIGG

Sharon Rigg was born in Cleveland, Ohio, and has since lived in Washington DC, Switzerland, and England. She now lives with her husband and two children in Surrey, where, in addition to writing, she teaches American literature in the TASIS school.

Also by Sharon Rigg
in Pan Books

The Recital

SHARON RIGG

Nickel Malley

PAN BOOKS
London, Sydney and Auckland

First published 1991 by
Pan Books Ltd, Cavaye Place, London SW10 9PG
9 8 7 6 5 4 3 2 1
© Sharon Rigg 1990
ISBN 0 330 31393 2

Printed in England by Clays Ltd, St Ives plc

For Lyle

With special thanks to
Carol Smith and Suzanne Baboneau

One

So much has hinged on Nickel Malley. The day the storm burst was the day her father was shot, and although I can remember exactly what I was doing when I heard that he had died, just as many people can recall what they were doing when they learned of President Kennedy's assassination, the other details of the day are blurred. There was one clear illumination in that day, one moment of a searchlight focused on a dead man, and then the plunge into darkness. It was not until I was tumbled into that darkness that I became uneasily aware that all that had preceded the event had become, or always had been, dim as well.

Perhaps equating Dan Malley's death with President Kennedy's is irreverent or fatuous. Dan's demise did not affect a nation or a world; to his family and his neighbours, though, his death was equally devastating. It compelled us to question our lives and our beliefs, and it uncovered some of our illusions, in much the same way that Kennedy's death did. It was a long, long time before people in Burton, New York, could wake up each morning and not question the solidity of the earth on which they stood, a long time before we did not all look askance at our neighbours and friends and wonder: *How could this happen in a town like ours? What else is going to descend to churn up our worlds?*

My mother, Sairy, has a saying which, for as long as I can remember, she has found occasion to use at least once each day. Her conversation is typically peppered

5

with maxims and proverbs and bits of folk wisdom, but this one saying was repeated so frequently that it became ingrained in me, embedded. It wore its way into my skull much as a steady drip of water will slowly bore a hole into a rock. I never questioned it; it was absorbed.

Her saying is, "Life's a book", to which she usually adds, "Daryl, you gotta keep turning those pages. It won't do any good to look back. Just keep turning those pages."

It seems harmless enough, this adage, but in retrospect, I see that it shaped me, and it was inevitable that I would defy it. I am stealthily turning back those pages, belatedly comprehending that I have missed pithy revelations which would have allowed me to foresee some of the stumbling blocks ahead, to be prepared for what was to come. Already, as I look back, I see a version of my younger self, the probing Daryl Wilson, racing along through an enormous tome, riffling through those pages of my life, pressing ahead to finish the chapter, begin the next, bolting on, much as I do when I read a good, well-plotted suspense story, eager to solve the mystery. It only occurs to me now that I have always been disappointed when I do skid to the close of those stories – not disappointed so much in how they terminate, but because I have to sever myself from that world and be hurled back into a world without answers and resolutions. Why have I been sprinting through my own "book" when the last page will be identical to everyone else's? What is the hurry?

I wonder if Dan Malley ever contemplated this, hurtling through his life, tearing through his pages, only to smack into his surprise ending, well before he knew it was coming.

I may regret this scrutiny of the past, but I am ill-suited to advance to any new chapters until I do. Perhaps scenes will be unearthed that will make it harder to forge on, or scenes that I would never have needed to know. It is at least a way to refrain from turning the current page, to postpone what is ahead. I am not in any haste to read the last one.

Two

Dan Malley seemed an amiable man, always toting one of his own children on his back or towing one by the hand, always the first to pitch in and help me shovel snow from the driveway after my father had his heart attack and had to be content to huddle by the front window and watch the world go by. In those years that my father had to "take it easy", we saw a lot of Dan Malley. He rescued our cat from a tree, mounted the roof and fastened loose shingles, painted the upper storey of our house, and whisked both me and my sister Jenny along with his own children camping.

There were four Malley children: Doug, Joey, Nickel and Danny Jr. I was closest in age to Joey, but nearest in temperament to Danny Jr, the one everyone said was "a little weird". My mother has always suggested that Danny Jr "listens to the beat of a different drum", but it was a beat that struck a familiar chord with me. The oldest Malley boy, Doug, was my sister Jenny's age – nearly sixteen when we first went camping with them. Camping was the last adventure Jenny would be intrigued by, and on that first trip, my mother had to force her to go. Thereafter, however, Jenny was not only willing, but practically fervid – yearning and impatient for those weekends to arrive, sullen and despondent when they

7

drew to a close. On these trips, she hovered around Doug or his father, much to my relief, for had she been bored, she would have taken out her misery on me.

For me, the lure of the trips was Danny, that "different" drummer, and of course, there was Nickel. I wasn't yet old enough to be infatuated, but, like most other people, I was mesmerized by her. Even on those earliest camping trips, when I was barely twelve and Nickel was only nine, she seemed to infect us all with a sense of promise and protection.

Nickel was extraordinary. I knew it before I became a part of that family – everyone in the town knew it. There was, paradoxically, both a shimmer and an enormous calm about her, and those eyes – ah. She could look into yours and transmit something other-worldly.

It seemed to me that the whole time she was growing up, she was being groomed to become a symbol of perfection, an almost Madonna-like figure of grace. Only now is it easy to see what a heavy mantle that would have been for anyone to bear, but it doesn't lessen the painful irony of the whirling abyss Nickel found herself the centre of later on.

My sister Jenny was the only person in the whole town, I think, who not only resisted Nickel's spell, but who couldn't bear the sight of Nickel Malley. Nickel sensed that, from the beginning. On the camping trips, Nickel would steer clear of Jenny, and, in turn, Jenny seemed determined to keep Mr Malley from his daughter Nickel's grasp.

Occasionally, I would watch the two girls exchange glances across the campfire. Nickel's gaze seemed to penetrate Jenny and accept her for what she was – at that time, an audacious flirt and self-centred teenager; Jenny's stare was malevolent, derisive, scornful. Perhaps it is only with hindsight, but I think I sensed even then that these two were sizing each other up as two boxers might, standing against the ropes, circling, pacing, preparing for the fight. How often, I wonder, does the referee for such a fight get trapped between the blows?

Mr Malley was fifteen or twenty years younger than my father and so he appeared, full of energy, vigorous, a model of virility. I can recall wishing, on more than one occasion, that he were my father, instead of the ageing, shuffling Barney Wilson. Everything about Dan seemed in contrast to my father. Dan's thick, dark brown hair and deep, dark eyes appeared dramatic compared to my father's thinning, grey hair and pale, hazel eyes. Dan was tall, muscular and solid; my father was short, stocky, flabby. Dan bounded into a room; my father crept cautiously. The voice of Dan Malley echoed and boomed; Barney Wilson's was faded and thinned. My father was not nearly so decrepit as this, but it is how I perceived him then, shadowed in the resplendent light of Dan Malley.

In short, Dan Malley was everything I wanted my own father to be, but I was young then and appearances were more important than substance. Dan was capable of acts my father wasn't, and that became Dan's undoing. Ironically, I didn't discover Dan's darker core until after he died, and I didn't discover my own father's luminosity until after his fatal stroke.

"Too early foolish, too late wise," my mother would say.

Burton, our simple town, nestles in a flat plain near the low, sloping foothills of Shadrach Mountain. The mountain is barely a hill, glimpsed vaguely off in the distance as a tree-covered rise. This corner of western New York state is dotted with small towns like ours, crossed with two state highways, off which stem all the roads and drives and avenues of modest Burton.

Here is a congenial collection of neighbourhoods, and while we know everyone within our own immediate neighbourhood, Burton boasts enough residents that one does not know everyone, though perhaps everyone looks vaguely familiar, having been glimpsed previously on Main Street or at the baseball park or the high school.

It is a town where people look twice at strangers, but with open curiosity, not hostility. There is a section for the rich, Blue Meadows, and a section for the poor, Wexley Road, but all the rest is populated by people like us – the Malleys and the Wilsons – our parents dwelling firmly in the middle class, employed in both blue-collar and white-collar jobs. Growing up, we were conscious of money and the need to conserve it, but we never went hungry and our parents could always pay the mortgage. Teenagers worked at odd jobs, many married right out of high school, perhaps half of us went to college, the rest went to work right away or joined the armed services, but it was clearly assumed that most of us would settle down right here in Burton when the time came. It hardly seems the sort of place where a man could be shot in his own back yard, surrounded by his family and friends.

Three

We lived on the same street as the Malleys, in nearly identical white frame houses. Our door, however, was blue; theirs was red. Our house was tidy inside; theirs was a layered concoction of jackets, boots, books, footballs, shoes. Often, after those long-ago camping trips, Dan Malley would drop off his own children at his house and escort me and Jenny home. Dan would sit at our kitchen table with my parents, drinking beer and talking, making the entire room warmer with his presence, his vitality. Usually, Jenny and I would linger in the kitchen, grateful for any excuse to extend our time with Dan Malley.

On one such evening, my mother mentioned Dan's "beautiful daughter Nickel", and Jenny, who had been leaning against the sink, pushing a Coca-Cola bottle back and forth across the counter and swaying her blue-jeaned fanny in time to a tune which only she could hear, suddenly thrust the bottle against the toaster and stormed out of the room. A brief silence followed, during which I crept to the other side of the refrigerator and slid to the floor, where I could hear but not be seen.

"I wish my Jenny were more like Nickel," my mother said.

"Now, Sairy," Mr Malley teased, "maybe my Nickel will turn out to be a real hellion one day – who knows?"

"No chance." My father's voice seemed toneless, languishing in the air, his words disintegrating in the wake of Dan Malley's sonorous speech.

My mother talked about the day Dan and Imogen brought Nickel home from the hospital. "Clear as anything, I remember it," she said. "She was lying there in a white wicker bassinet and lord, I was just hypnotized. I couldn't quit staring at her."

"She have dribble on her face or something?" That was Dan, a joker, not one to be drawn into this dreamy portrait. Or so I thought.

"Hush. It was her skin, the most beautiful colour in this whole world – the palest, purest pink of a perfect rose, the inside petals, the velvety soft ones that make you want to weep they are so perfect. Her skin seemed as delicate and fragile as those petals – or as the wing of a butterfly." My mother, often the realist in the family, can easily veer off

11

into romantic byways, but it was a fitting description, I thought, of Nickel's skin.

I think it was that same night that I first heard something new and curious in Dan Malley's voice. He said, "Don't laugh—" and of course my mother and father both laughed. "I mean it," he said, and he waited for them to take him seriously. There was something in his voice that I couldn't identify then, but now it seems that it might have been vulnerability. Whatever it was, it frightened me. He said, "I used to reach in and touch that skin, and when I put my hand against her cheek – don't laugh – my finger looked so yellow, wrinkled and old, and I used to think, *my life is over*."

I remember looking down at my own fingers then, at the dirt embedded beneath the nails and at the droplets of dried blood scattered along scratches etched into the backs of my hands.

My parents didn't laugh. Instead, my mother's voice dropped to match Dan's and she confessed that when she first saw Nickel, she "might as well have been seeing Jesus Christ himself in the manger".

"Good Lord!" Dan said.

"Well, it's true," my mother said. "She's no normal kid."

I tried to superimpose Nickel's face on an image I had of the baby Jesus, lying in the manger wrapped in swaddling clothes, gazing peacefully upward at the Wise Men. I could see the Wise Men's expressions, awed, reflecting the baby's own radiance. Nickel's eyes reminded me of smooth, round, brown chestnuts that have just emerged from their shells. The contrast between their former covering, their prickly shell, and their newborn shimmer always seemed rather miraculous to me. My mother would have said, "Things, Daryl, are not always what they seem," suggesting that of course

12

beauty hid beneath ugly wrappings. But did it also mean the reverse?

I have never been able to look directly at Nickel's eyes for more than a few seconds. Rays of white light bounce off them, straight at you, as if you are getting messages from God himself. But my sister Jenny has always said that Nickel has "devil eyes". We fought about this once, with me yelling that Nickel had God's eyes, and Jenny swearing they were the devil's, and Jenny pinching my arm while I tried to scratch her face. Our mother intervened. She said, and not for the first or last time, "You see what you are," but it was probably another five years before I knew what she meant.

In the kitchen that night, though, Dan continued talking in that low, haunting voice. "When I first held Nickel in the hospital, she opened her eyes and I had to look away. On the wall was a mirror. My eyes looked streaky and mucky; the whites were striped with yellow and red, like an old dirty handkerchief. It depressed me. I thought: *Where has the time gone? What is left for you, Dan Malley?*

That was when I left the kitchen. Although I was intrigued by talk about Nickel's skin and her eyes, I did not like Dan's voice. The sorrow in it frightened me, and I did not want to hear that Dan Malley could feel depressed. I did not want to hear about his mucky eyes. So I went upstairs and, lying on my bed, I recreated the picture of Dan Malley by the campfire, grinning, eyes sparkling, voice hearty and resonant. That Dan Malley, the one by the campfire, was my hero, not the one who seemed to feel that the birth of his beautiful daughter was a sign of his own mortality.

Four

Although it is difficult to be objective about Nickel, because I have always been in awe of her, it is even more difficult to be objective about my sister, Jenny. We quarrelled and collided all the way through our childhood; she was always my wretched older sister, the one who caused me perpetual pain and embarrassment. It was a shock to see her emerge from college married (it was beyond my comprehension that any man would *choose* to live with her) and qualified to return to Burton High as a teacher. It must have been something of a jolt to her, too, to face in the classroom her former neighbours and little brother's friends.

Suddenly all those "younger brats", as she called them, were her students and she was Mrs Maple Branch (the name still sounds absurd to me), transfigured into, apparently, a benevolent, affable teacher. I escaped her classroom through either good fortune or the guidance counsellor's good sense, but others didn't. In her third year of teaching, Jenny reigned over, among others, Nickel Malley and Mick MacNeil, and it was an experience that altered all three of them.

I had heard of Maple Branch, as had everyone in our high school, for Maple had been one of Burton High's All-Star state football champions. In the trophy case outside the gymnasium were framed articles about him, accompanied by pictures of Maple in his football uniform, shoulder pads hunched around his neck, his round, boyish face attempting a menacing look for the camera. In some, he held a football aloft, his massive hands making the ball appear like a child's toy. In others, he crouched threateningly.

This was the sort of boy Jenny had always preferred. She appreciated muscles; she sought out strong, sturdy physiques. In high school, she dated most of the football team, Maple among them, but it wasn't until Maple returned from a four-year stint in the Army that they began dating seriously. Although he had the star athlete's swagger, his time in the Army had apparently calmed him somewhat. Previously known as a beer-drinking carouser, he returned more guarded and quiet. Once married to Jenny, his hardened muscles quickly gave way to soft fat, and he began to resemble more a cuddly bear than the fierce competitor that his pictures in the trophy case suggested.

Because he now appeared so gentle and harmless, with his increasingly rounded face and belly, it was difficult to imagine him either as a former football star or as the insensitive, tempestuous person about whom Jenny increasingly complained. Maple basked for a long time in the reflected glory of his high school days, but I supposed that sooner or later that might begin to wane, and he would seek this attention from his wife. Jenny, however, was not one to share the spotlight with another.

If I rummage deep enough, I can recall times when Jenny befriended me. She helped me with my homework, but that usually resulted in her slapping me on the arm, calling me stupid and thick-headed, so it seemed all the more curious that she became a teacher. I had never known Jenny to be long on patience; she insisted on the last word on everything.

If she was told to clean her room, she'd say, "I *know*." And if my mother said, "I mean it," Jenny would say, "I *know*." They would go on and on like that, until my mother would say, "JENNY MAE WILSON, YOU CAN'T ALWAYS HAVE THE LAST WORD!" Jenny would turn, leave the room, and when she was just barely out of my mother's earshot, Jenny would say, "I *know*!"

Once, on a camping trip, she backed Nickel up against the tent and said, "Nickel. Nickel. Stupid name!"

Nickel blinked, widening those spectacular eyes at my sister. "Is not," she said.

"Nickel. Nickel. How'd you ever get a stupid name like that?"

Nickel was not intimidated. "It's really Nicole."

"Nicole? Nicole? Oh, how la-dee-dah! Oh, how very French! If it's Nicole, why doesn't anyone call you Nicole? Huh? Huh?"

Nickel did not respond; she stood there gazing at Jenny until Jenny whirled and stomped away. That night, around the campfire, Jenny asked Mr Malley, "Is her name really Nicole?" The name slid out of Jenny's mouth as if it were distasteful, bitter. Jenny was standing behind Mr Malley, leaning against his back as he added logs to the campfire.

He had the rugged looks of a cowboy, I thought: strong jaw, ruddy complexion, thick hair, lean but muscular body. "Sure is," he said.

"Then why don't you *call* her Nicole? Why do you call her Nickel?"

Jenny, at sixteen, did not often touch our own father affectionately, so it seemed surprising to me that she could lean against Dan Malley this way. She behaved, with Dan Malley, more as she did with boys her age, touching, flirting, wiggling, always moving.

He said, "Would Quarter have been better?"

"Hah! Funn-eeee."

"We couldn't find a name for her. People kept suggesting names like Hope or Angel or Mercy – can you see me saying, 'Hey, Hope, you stop that snivelling?'"

"Ha, ha."

"We could see from the start that no normal name would fit—"

Jenny pushed against his back, throwing him off balance so that he had to brace both hands against the ground to keep from falling into the fire.

"No offence—" he said. He sat back, cross-legged. Jenny leaned in front of him, retrieving a log and tossing it into the fire. "I can see down your shirt," he said.

Jenny smirked, leaned forward, pulled Dan Malley's shirt toward her and said, "I can see down yours, too." She sat beside him. "You still haven't said how you came up with that name."

Dan had this habit of putting his right hand up to his chest, slipping his fingers inside his shirt, rubbing the skin over his heart. It was a gesture that later, when I read *The Scarlet Letter*, reminded me of Reverend Dimmesdale's repeated, guilty gesture. He was doing this now, rubbing his chest. "Imogen said she'd like a nice, pure, French name, you know, like Simone or Nicole. We settled on Nicole. But when we got her home, Joey and Doug thought we were saying 'Nickel'. That's what they called her and it just stuck. So instead of a nice, pure name, she's got just a plain old Nickel name."

"It's not plain," Jenny said, obviously jealous, but she recovered. "It's just stupid."

Dan Malley turned and smiled at her. I thought at the time what a gentle person he was to ignore her jealousy and her rudeness, to like her even though she hadn't earned it. It seems a bit sad to realize that I was like Jenny in this way, thinking you had to earn or win affection from others – or at least from those who weren't your parents. And although we took our parents' devotion for granted and abused it, we worked at earning it from teachers, from our peers, from just about everyone except Dan

17

Malley, because he gave his affections easily. Too easily, I now realize.

Perhaps Jenny was a normal teenager, but it seemed to me that she strutted and preened her way through adolescence like a prima donna in a lead role. She had long, fine, fly-away hair, reddish-blonde like my father's used to be, and she constantly flung her hair this way and that, tossing her head, shaking her mane. She wore tight jeans, skimpy T-shirts and bright bracelets; she flounced and wiggled, showing off her backside, leaning over so you could see down her shirt, all the while fluttering her arms and jangling her bracelets. If she was anywhere near by you knew it. You couldn't miss her. My mother once said she was going to chain Jenny to her bedpost in order to get her through those years. She also used to tell her, "Still water is a lot more enticing than a heaving whirlpool."

Although Nickel was seven years younger than Jenny, she seemed to have always offered the enticement of "still water". She possessed elegance, grace and poise. She had thick, glossy, black hair; she moved slowly, purposely, lithely, rather like a ballerina or an aery spirit. While Jenny squirmed and bounced, Nickel might lean against a tree, curling into it as if she were part of it. She ran with the grace of a gazelle, was a natural athlete but not competitive. She seemed apparently diffident to the attention she attracted, having neither sought it nor expected it, unaware of her powers.

If I were the only one who thought of Nickel in these lofty terms, I would put it down to infatuation. But everyone – except Jenny, that is – saw Nickel this way. On the eve of my marriage to Nickel, my mother said, "Treat her like she's holy, Daryl," and that reminded me of something I had heard my mother say to my father once, long before the shooting. She had said,

"Barney, when that girl looks at me, I feel like I'm getting some kind of message, maybe even a judgement, from something holy. But she also makes me feel *mortal*. I come away vowing to be a better person and to do some good in this world while I still have some days left. I come home and I want to weed the garden and bring flowers in the house and wash my hair and slather on Noxema and be nice to the kids."

After the shooting, though, most people wondered how something that beautiful, something that made people so aware of promises and possibilities – how could that cause so much destruction?

My mother said, "It turns the world upside down, it does."

Five

I first heard about Mick, the boy who became so closely associated with Nickel and the one who took the blame for Dan Malley's death, from Jenny. I was home from university for a long weekend. This was the year that Jenny taught both Nickel and Mick in her English class.

Jenny, making her token visit to welcome me home, was ensconced at the kitchen table grading papers. Maple chopped wood in the back yard, I was finishing a late breakfast, and my mother was fluttering around the kitchen. Although she still wore her trademark bracelets which clanged against the table as she worked, Jenny had abandoned her blue jeans in favour of a skin-tight red skirt and had exchanged her skimpy T-shirt for a silky blouse, leaving the top three buttons undone. Holding one of her students' papers aloft, she said, "Listen to this. This boy is amazing."

"Which boy?"

"Henry MacNeil. The kids call him Mick."

"Carl and Liza's son?" my mother asked. "I thought all those boys were hoodlums."

Jenny tossed her hair back. "The older boys are! I taught one last year, one the year before. But this one, Mick, is different. You know what he wrote last week? An essay about himself and this one line, I'll never forget. He said, 'Sometimes I like to just lie back in the grass, stare at the sky, and contemplate what to wear tomorrow and the meaning of life.' Nice, huh?"

My mother said, "Isn't that just like a kid? To them, it's just as big a deal deciding what to wear tomorrow as what in the world life is all about."

"Maple says they don't think beyond their own noses."

"Hunh," snorted Sairy. "Maybe that's because *he* doesn't."

"Ma—"

"You know I'm just teasing. You know I love Maple to death. After all, he's sure done a good job at taming *you*."

"Ha, ha. What are *you* laughing at, Daryl?"

"Nothing."

"Anyway," Jenny said, "another line I remember was in an essay on loneliness. Mick wrote that he didn't like the 'sound of his own breathing filling up the room'. Don't you like the way he puts things?"

I had to admit he sounded a cut above the ordinary high school boy.

"So this paper," Jenny said as she shook it in front of her, jangling her bracelets, "was supposed to be about how they reacted to a crisis. They had to describe what the crisis was and how they reacted to it." Jenny proceeded to

20

read, her voice conforming to the soft, personal tone of Mick's essay.

I was intrigued by what she read, but it also unnerved me. He seemed too sensitive, too revealing, too vulnerable for a sixteen-year-old boy. He wore no protective mask. At that age, I would have rather died than divulge some of the feelings Mick did. It wasn't that he revealed anything outrageous, and it wasn't about sex. His "crisis" was the time his good friend moved away. They had been friends for ten years, and when his friend left, Mick felt abandoned. He felt worse, he said, than if his own parents had walked out on him.

For three days, he refused to leave his room, he refused food, and he refused to speak. Finally, his father called Dr Feeter, who tried to reason with Mick. Mick bit his hand. Dr Feeter advised Mick's father to "slap him upside the head".

Then, on the fourth day, while Mick was lying in bed, half-starved to death and wishing he *were* dead, a bumblebee flew in his window. Mick said, in his paper, that he didn't know what came over him, that he started swatting at the bumblebee and smashing it, and even when he had squished it against the wall, he kept beating it and beating it until his father appeared and grabbed ahold of him. Mick started crying, and he cried and cried like a baby. Then the next day he got up, ate breakfast, and never thought about his friend again. Not, he said, until he wrote this paper.

I never would have admitted crying.

But that wasn't all. Mick said that it was not until right then when he was writing about it that he started remembering all the good times they had shared and how his friend used to smile and how his teeth were so perfect and white. And Mick realized, while he was writing that paper, that the bumblebee was somehow a substitute for his friend, that he wanted to kill the friend for leaving him. And he also said that he was ashamed to realize that he, Mick, was so bad inside.

I certainly would never have said those things to a *teacher*.

I was uncomfortable when she finished reading, convinced that Jenny was going to laugh at Mick and at what he had written. But I forgot that this was the new, transformed Jenny, the one who had found compassion somewhere, either in college or with Maple Branch.

Jenny wrote something at the bottom of his paper, and I walked around behind her to see what she had written. I was surprised. She wrote, "Don't feel bad, we all have something wretched inside us, but most of us aren't ever noble enough to admit it."

I patted her shoulder. "Well, well, well," I said. "Miss Compassionate. Amazing."

She slapped my hand away.

She read through a few more papers while I finished breakfast. Suddenly, she said, "God! Will you look at this?" She held up a paper with only two sentences written on it. Nickel Malley's name was at the top.

Nickel had written, "There must be something wrong with me, because I have never had a crisis. I'm sorry."

"Well," my mother said.

"Well, nothing!" retorted Jenny. "Can you imagine that? A sixteen-year-old girl who has never had a crisis? She's spoiled to death, I tell you. The goddam Queen of Sheba!"

"Now, Jenny—"

"Don't you 'now, Jenny', me. Don't you think someone ought to worry about a sixteen-year-old girl who's never had a crisis?"

My mother took a long look at Jenny. "And don't you think that someone ought to worry about a boy who

22

would beat an ole bumblebee to death and bite Dr Feeter just because his friend moved away?"

Someone knocked at the back door. "Why, it's Dan Malley," my mother said. "Put that paper away, Jenny, and keep your mouth shut about Nickel or—"

"I *know*," Jenny said.

"Hey," Dan boomed. "Ready to fix that garage door, Daryl?"

Jenny was already preening. She had buried Nickel's paper in the stack of essays and was tossing her hair off her shoulders and fidgeting with the buttons on her blouse as the bracelets clicked and jingled.

I leaned over and whispered to her, "You're *married*, dear."

She slapped my arm again. "Shut *up*."

My mother asked what Imogen Malley was doing. Dan leaned against the refrigerator and slid his fingers inside his shirt, rubbing at his chest. "Worrying, what else?" He laughed.

"What is it this time?"

"Oh you know, any little thing. Actually, I think she's worrying because she read an article that said parents don't always worry about the kid they ought to worry about."

"Huh?"

"Yeah, so Imogen is sitting there worrying that maybe she hasn't been worrying about the right one. She's spent her whole life worrying about Doug and Joey and Danny, but now she thinks maybe she should have been worrying about Nickel! Imagine!"

Jenny and my mother exchanged knowing looks. Jenny then stood, having a sudden need to retrieve something from the refrigerator, something on a low shelf so that she could stick out her fanny. "Want anything, Dan?" she asked.

23

"Sure," he said.

"Ha, ha." Jenny poked him in the ribs.

"Now your mother's going to get some bad ideas there, Jenny."

My mother was watching all right, but more in fear that Jenny would embarrass us all than that Dan Malley might suggest anything inappropriate.

It occurred to me then that had my parents been younger – had they been closer to Dan's and Imogen's ages, my mother and Dan Malley would have made a better pair than Imogen and Dan. In fact, I thought, Imogen and my father would also have made a suitable pair. They should have switched, I thought.

My mother, Sairy, was animated, open, robust. She and Dan both enjoyed – even relished – children and laughed readily. My father, quiet, serious and lethargic since his heart attack nearly ten years before, lived each day as if it would be his last – and I don't mean he lived it to the hilt – he waited for Death's knock, brooding in his chair, leaden and moribund, guarding each breath.

Dan was not overstating Imogen's worrying. It seemed she was endlessly wrestling with some pressing problem, which she would discuss with my mother, whom she had adopted as an older mentor. "Sairy," she would say, "what do you think about—" or "What should I do about—" or "How should I—" as if she were incapable of assessing or deciding anything for herself. At times one could detect shadows of Nickel's striking beauty in Imogen's face, but that was only in rare moments when Imogen was relaxed. More often, Imogen's skin appeared taut, her cheekbones hollow, her skin dull. Nickel had inherited Dan's round, huge, dark eyes (although Nickel's were even rounder, bigger and darker), not her mother's which were small and

24

hazel, the eyelids rimmed in pink. She looked as if she had a perpetual allergy or as if she had recently been crying.

But then, I supposed, perhaps these two couples were well paired after all; perhaps opposites do attract and do endure, bonded by their very differences. Although I would not have perceived it then, now I see that two shining stars make a poor pair; each is accustomed to soaking up reflected glory, and neither desires to share it. It seems that one always has to outshine the other, who serves, either willingly or resentfully, as the foil or the backdrop.

I felt, after my father died, that there was more to his "backdrop" than I had been aware. For some time after his death, my mother lost her footing, unsure of her place and her role without the silent passivity of my father to reflect her own liveliness. Likewise, when Dan Malley died, Imogen nearly faded into the woodwork, her mind in complete disarray.

"Oh," Dan said, "Sairy, I almost forgot. Imogen wants to know if you'll come by and help her lay out a dress pattern."

"Oh? For herself?"

"For Nickel. Big dance coming up. First real date."

Jenny rolled her eyes at me. I knew she was thinking "Queen of Sheba" again.

I was stunned when Dan said "first real date". I had almost convinced myself that Nickel was too pure or too seraphic to become enmeshed in that whole process of dating, or perhaps I felt that she had suddenly grown up when I had not been looking, or perhaps I was purely jealous.

I had kept some distance from Nickel in the last few years, presuming that she was too splendid for the likes of me, that she would never condescend to be linked romantically with me. Besides, she frightened me; marked power was contained in those eyes; she seemed to know vastly more than I, and surely she would expose me if I gave her the chance.

This was all supposition, of course. Nickel had never done anything to merit these rather harsh judgements. She did not flaunt any lofty wisdom; when I was with her, she was more the listener than the talker. And she certainly never "exposed" people; rather, she seemed, if I were to be completely honest, to accept people for what they were and to appreciate, even savour, what she beheld.

"You see what you are," as my mother said. So I suppose that then, at least, I was fearful and unsure of women, manipulative of others, judgemental. And I surely would have been outraged if anyone had brought those flaws to my attention, instead of unearthing them for myself!

"First date!" my mother said. "Oh!"

"How marvellous," Jenny said, drily.

"With whom?" I asked. "Anyone we know?"

"Mick. Know him? MacNeil."

"The bumblebee boy!" I said, too quickly.

"Shut *up*!" Jenny said, reaching across the table to smack my arm.

"What?" said Dan.

"Honest to God, Daryl—" Jenny was shoving the essays into a folder.

"Bumblebee?" Dan said.

Six

The next time I was home for a visit that year, the year before Dan Malley was shot, was Christmas vacation, and it was during this time that I first saw Mick with Nickel.

"You should see them," my mother had said, "what a lovely pair. He *idolizes* her, can't take his eyes off her. They're a perfect match. Perfect."

We were sitting in the living room. My father, immersed in his overstuffed chair, was pitching popcorn out the window.

"Isn't it a little *cold* in here?" I asked.

"Now, Daryl, he can't very well throw the popcorn out the window with it *closed*, now can he?"

"Why is he tossing popcorn out the window anyway?"

"Daryl. Shh. He's not invisible, you know. He's not deaf. He can hear you. Can't you, Barney? Barney?"

"Of course," my father answered.

Dan Malley had affectionately nicknamed my father "Verbless Barney" years ago, long before his heart attack. Never even remotely verbose, my father habitually omitted verbs from his sentences. It seemed fitting, somehow, that action be absent even from his speech.

"Dad, why are you throwing popcorn out the window?"

"Birds."

"Ah, of course. Birds." Two or three blackbirds were swooping in and out of the oak tree, scooping up the corn.

"I didn't realize you liked birds so much."

"Always."

"Ah."

My mother said, "You should see him, Daryl."

"Pardon?" I thought she was referring to my father, who was sitting in plain sight before me.

"Mick. You know. Mick with Nickel. What a pair."

"I know. 'Perfect,' you said."

"He follows her everywhere. He's sitting on their doorstep in the morning, waiting for her, and he walks her to school, and after school, you can see them downtown, and then he walks her home, and he studies over there. What a pair."

"Mmm."

Even my father was in on it. "Peas in a pod," he said.

"Mmm."

"I met him. Mick. I met him over at Imogen's. What a nice boy. He's so very tall. You should see him. I was over at Imogen's, sitting in the kitchen, and in walks Nickel and then right behind her, like a shadow, was this glorious tall boy with curly black hair and ebony eyes. Wasn't there a song, *Ebony Eyes*? Barney?"

"Eh?"

"Wasn't there a song, *Ebony Eyes*?" She hummed a few bars.

"Maybe so," he said. He cast a whole fistful of popcorn out the window.

It was mighty cold in that room.

"And Nickel just walked right up and introduced us, just like that, very politely, you know how she is. 'Mrs Wilson, I'd like you to meet Mick MacNeil. Mick, this is Mrs Wilson.' And he stepped up and shook my hand. Very firmly, but not too firmly. Firmly, but gently, I'd say. What a nice boy."

"Mmm."

"Your sister Jenny never would have done that. She would have rather jumped off a bridge than bring some boy into the house to be introduced to a stranger. She would have been antsy and squirming to get out of the house before anybody could examine him. Not Nickel, though. As calm as you please, she—"

"Popcorn?" my father asked. His bowl was empty.

28

"I'll make it," I said.

In the kitchen, my mother asked, "Why don't you bring any girls home, Daryl? Hmm?"

I did not know, really. I had dated enough girls, but it had never occurred to me to bring them home. What would I do with them once we arrived? It seemed to me you had to know a girl tolerably well to be able to casually bring her home and let her see how you lived when you weren't with her, bedecked in your different face.

This was also when I was bounding through my "sampling" phase. I squandered girls rather quickly, exhausting their possibilities (or my own) in a few weeks, maybe a few months; then either I lost interest, or the girl lost interest, or someone else looked intriguing and off I veered in hot pursuit. The "chase" was much more thrilling to me than what followed. I dreaded that point at which you begin to repeat yourself, or she repeats herself, or you run out of gay, novel things to do, and discover yourself one evening, languid, frankly bored.

I also instinctively panicked whenever a girl would say, "What should we do Saturday then?" taking it for granted that we would of course be doing *something* together a week hence. An immature reaction, I know, but that's how I was. I suppose I had an encapsulated vision of precisely what I was seeking, and I nibbled at various varieties, tentatively, testing. I did not really know until later that I was holding each girl up to the light of Nickel Malley, and of course no one could match that ideal.

I was not a Don Juan, though. I was not all brash confidence. I sweated over asking girls out, worried that they might say no, gave considerable thought to what I should wear and how I should comb my hair and what I should say and when I should kiss and when or if I should fondle and when or if I should take them to bed. But although I fretted over these things, this was the exciting part: determining the signals, the rules, the parameters. It was, I hate to concede, rather like a game.

That Christmas holiday, when I first saw Mick and Nickel, I was in my second year at university and only beginning to wonder, as I watched some of my friends make "commitments" (a commitment was remaining faithful to one girl for more than six months), whether I would ever find someone with whom I wouldn't panic when she said, "Well, then, what should we do next Saturday?"

And I was increasingly aware that whenever I was bedded down with my current "sample", I would inevitably think of Nickel Malley and two particular camping trips.

The first trip that I would recall was when I was about thirteen, Nickel ten. Jenny no longer joined us on these trips, being off at university herself then. Dan Malley had set up two tents. He, Joey and Nickel were to sleep in one, Danny and I in the other. But after dinner that night, Danny vomited over the picnic table, and his father put him in his own tent, to keep an eye on him. Nickel offered to sleep in mine.

We were very young, enormously innocent, and so of course no one thought twice about it. That night, rain poured for hours and I awoke, uncomfortably damp. My sleeping bag had been touching the sides of the tent and the water had seeped through and drenched it. I took off my clothes, found a pair of dry jeans but no shirt, and nudged Nickel. "My sleeping bag's all wet," I said.

She didn't say anything, merely unzipped her sleeping bag and held it open. It did not for a moment occur to me that there was anything improper about this. I crawled in and she turned toward me and rested her head on my shoulder, curving against me. Immediately, I was hard. Nickel moved closer. "Oh," she said, looking up at me.

I think I said something like, "It's OK, go to sleep," which she did, but I lay there clinging to her, absolutely hypnotized, stunned by this new feeling and dreading its inevitable diminishment.

I was awakened the next morning by Dan Malley, who was standing in our tent. "Hey!" he said. "What in the world—?"

I scrambled out of the sleeping bag much too fast, looking guilty, I am sure. "My sleeping bag – wet – the rain—" I said, as I clumsily held the wet bag aloft for inspection.

Dan Malley had such a frightening look on his face – frightening to me, that is. He looked as if he was going to thrash me, and in my absolute naïvety, I thought it was because I had let the sleeping bag, which belonged to the Malleys, get wet. I was so intent on apologizing about the wet bag and offering to have it cleaned and on and on, that Dan Malley finally had to laugh. My innocence was confirmed, it seemed, by my failure to even remotely suspect why he might really be angry. Nickel slept on.

The next time I found myself sharing a sleeping bag with Nickel was three years later, when I was sixteen, Nickel thirteen. I hadn't been camping with the Malleys for over a year. Again, it was Dan Malley, Joey, Danny, Nickel and I. On this occasion, fate intervened again. Near dinner time of our first day, Doug arrived to fetch his father. Imogen had collapsed at home, falling down half a flight of stairs; she was in the hospital. At first, Dan Malley was going to pack us all up and take us with him, but Danny raised such a fuss, insisting that we were old enough to take care of ourselves and surely we could

31

spend one night here alone. His father could retrieve us the next day.

Dan Malley tried to convince Nickel to go with him, but she prevailed on him, in her calm, beguiling manner. "What could happen to me?" she said.

Although at first we were exhilarated with our freedom, we soon discovered that without Dan Malley's jovial, robust impetus, we were rather a lacklustre group, finding it difficult to amuse ourselves. We hadn't given any thought to sleeping arrangements. Again, there were two tents. Joey settled in one early on and was fast asleep as Danny, Nickel and I made feeble attempts at ghost stories around the fire. Soon, Nickel went in the other tent. Danny and I spent a long time talking. I think this is when he told me, "My dad is funny about Nickel." In his hands was a small box with holes punched in the lid. He opened it and lifted out a monarch butterfly.

"What do you mean?"

"He likes her better than us."

"That's just because she's a girl," I ventured.

"I know, but he still likes her better. He treats her like a glass ornament or something, always protecting her and polishing her."

"Polishing?"

"Polishing. You know, like this." He stroked the butterfly's reddish-brown wings.

"It won't be able to fly if you do that."

He ignored this. "My mother gets really mad."

"She does?"

"She tells him, 'She's not made of *glass*, Dan.'" Danny could do such wonderful impersonations. He tilted his head just as Imogen does and his voice took on that thin, whining quality hers has at times.

Danny said, "Where do you want to sleep?"

"Doesn't matter," I said, and at the moment it didn't.

"We could both sleep with Joey," he said.

"And leave Nickel alone?"

"She's not made of *glass*," Danny said, imitating his mother.

"I know, but your father – wouldn't he mind if we left her —"

"OK, then, you go with Nickel, I'll go with Joey. No big deal," he said, and we went to our respective tents.

I stripped to T-shirt and shorts and crawled into my sleeping bag. It was cold that night and my breath hung in the air. I had just closed my eyes, when Nickel said, "Daryl? You awake?" She was looking at me with those big, wide eyes. "Are you cold?" she said.

"Yes, it's freezing!"

"I know."

"Do you want my sweater?" I offered.

"No. That's OK."

I fell asleep. Some time later, though, I was awakened by Nickel, who was patting me on the shoulder. "Daryl, I'm so cold—" and so I unzipped my bag and she crawled in. She was wearing a long T-shirt which came to her knees and yes, she was cold. I rubbed her arms and pulled her up against me, but this time I sensed that maybe I should not be doing this. Her head was pressed against me and I could feel her breath on my chest.

"I can hear your heart," she said. And shortly, "I can feel your – uh – your—"

"Mmm," I said. "Well. I can't help it." I tried not to move, but I felt as if I would burst, straddling both heaven and hell all at once.

"Joey says it's not good for girls to make boys hard unless they're willing to do something about it," she said.

"God, Nickel!"

"I'm just telling you what Joey says. Should I go back to my sleeping bag?" She was complete innocence. I was convinced that if Jenny, at Nickel's age, had found herself in a sleeping bag with a boy, she would have known exactly what she was doing, but I knew that Nickel did not.

"Stay here," I said. I did not have much self control. I remember thinking, "I'll just kiss the top of her head," which I did. Then I thought, "I'll just rub her arms some more," which I did. But then it was no longer a rational process. Soon we were kissing each other and stroking each other, and how we got our clothes off inside that sleeping bag, I don't know, but we seemed to remove them with such grace. I promised her that I wouldn't do anything, that I wouldn't "stick it in", I think I said, or some equally foolish thing.

She said, "Oh, this is nice." She seemed quite intrigued by it all, but not hungry or ravenous, as I was. I came against her soft belly, apologizing afterward for the "mess", and she said, "Oh, it's all right. It was very nice. Really." And she fell asleep.

I lay awake the entire night, cradling her as if she were indeed "made of glass". I did not care to sleep; I dreaded the morning; I was madly, madly in love with Nickel Malley.

But I was reluctantly up and dressed at first light, terrified that Joey or Danny might discover us naked together, or worse yet, that Dan Malley would surprise us. I built a fire, walked to the lake, stood for a long time contemplating the magnificent universe in all my adolescent sentimentality, and felt as if the world had just opened up a huge, golden door to me.

That feeling dissolved rather quickly, for when I returned to the camp, Dan Malley was there, rousing Joey, Danny and Nickel, telling them that we all had to return home. Imogen was better, but confined to bed, and he was needed at home. I was terrified that he would question the previous night's sleeping arrangements or discover

Nickel sleeping naked, but by some good fortune, he seemed more intent on packing up the car and leaving quickly.

I had rehearsed exactly how I would look at Nickel when I first saw her that morning and what I might say, but fool that I was, I avoided her completely, mortified that Dan Malley would know what we had done. I felt certain that he would beat me to a pulp or banish me from their house, even though I had never seen him lose his temper and had never seen him strike one of his own children.

Nickel and I finally did exchange glances as we were getting into the car. She was so composed, so calm, as if nothing had happened, that it threw me off balance. By some irony, we ended up seated next to each other in the back seat, Nickel between me and Danny. Her arm pressed against mine and I thought I would leap out of the window, it was driving me so mad. I kept a magazine over my lap.

But now, in the kitchen, my mother interrupted my reverie. She was pressing the issue about my not bringing home any girls. "Will you, Daryl?"

"Will I what?"

"Bring someone home? Will you? You're not ashamed of us, are you?" She could adopt, at a moment's notice, her hurt-and-offended look.

"I'll think about it," I offered, not at all sure whom I might ask and what I would do with her once I got her here. I had been dating a girl named Judy, a wacky redhead. Perhaps she could help me make popcorn.

"Oh!" my mother said. "There they are!" She was pointing out the window.

There, strolling past our driveway, headed toward the Malleys' house, were Nickel and, I guessed, Mick. They had their backs to us, but I knew from the way he gazed down on her and from my mother's description of his shock of curly black hair that this must be Mick.

"Perfect," my mother said. She sighed.

Later that day, she said, "Daryl, come on with me over to the Malleys. They'll want to see you. You haven't been over there yet, have you?"

"No."

We went. On the way over to their house, my mother filled me in on the Malley family. Imogen hadn't been well, but she often wasn't well, so this was no surprise. "Dan's the same," she said, "good old Dan, he keeps that family hopping, he does." Doug was in the Air Force and "looked terrific in his uniform". Joey, like me, was in his second year at university, but he wasn't due home for another week. Danny Jr was "into art" and also into all kinds of trouble at school. In fact, my mother said, he was probably at school now – even though it wasn't in session – because he had to repaint the walls in one of the hallways. He had spray-painted a "suggestive mural" on them, and his punishment was to efface his mural with a coat of paint.

"Doesn't sound as if anyone's going to be home," I said.

"Imogen will be there, maybe Dan too, and of course," she said, "Nickel might be there."

Ah, Nickel.

I let Imogen and Dan fuss over me in the kitchen, accepting their comments on how much taller I was and how adult I looked and how handsome. "Driving the girls crazy?" Dan said, poking me in the ribs.

"Hardly," I answered.

"I can't get him to bring anybody home," my mother said. "He hides them from us."

"I wish Nickel would hide Mick sometimes," Dan said.

36

"Dan!" Imogen was sitting at the table, her chin resting in her hands. The rims of her eyes were red, as usual, her hair pulled back from her face, adding to her gaunt look.

And just then, Nickel came into the kitchen, followed by a long, lanky boy. Nickel looked stunning: her skin glowed, her dark hair shone, and God, those eyes. "Daryl!" She embraced me, kissed my cheek, stood back to appraise me. Mick edged closer to Nickel. "This is Mick," she said. "Mick, this is Daryl Wilson." She looked from one to the other of us, equally proud, it seemed, of each of us.

My parents were right; they did make quite a pair, with their stunning good looks, dark hair and dark eyes. There was a brooding, serious quality to Mick's expression, however, and he seemed guarded in our company, anxious to remove Nickel and be alone with her. He didn't touch her, but stood very close, watching her and taking cues from her expressions and actions. If she smiled, he did – although in weak imitation; if she moved, he did.

Dan leaned against the sink, rubbing his chest, and it seemed to me that his expression was one of tolerance or repressed annoyance. I gathered that he was not overly fond of Mick, but I remembered Mick's essays, and I could understand Mick's apparent infatuation with Nickel. I was almost sympathetic. But I also found myself irritated and annoyed. I had a quick vision of myself, whisking Nickel off on a white charger and galloping into the clichéd sunset.

Meanwhile, both my mother and Imogen unabashedly beamed at Mick and Nickel.

I made excuses to leave, and Nickel followed me to the front door, with Mick shadowing her. "I haven't seen you in so long," she said, and she put her hand against my ribs, an affectionate gesture which I had often seen her make toward her brothers and her father. Nonetheless, it had the effect of reducing me to jelly. Mick hovered inches away, watching my face.

I wanted to be witty and dynamic, and I wanted Mick to disappear, but for some reason, I said, "Well, I've been busy," and I left, with Nickel appearing a bit puzzled at the door and Mick clearly relieved.

Once home, I phoned Judy and asked her to a movie. I thought I might even bring her home with me afterwards.

Seven

"Daryl, I don't see why you couldn't have told me sooner. I don't see why you couldn't give me some notice. I have to take Barney over to Dr Feeter's, and I won't have time to bake any dessert and—"

"We don't need dessert. We don't even need dinner. We're going to a movie. I'm only bringing her here first because you made such a fuss about my not bringing anyone home."

The escapade with Judy was a fiasco from start to finish.

Judy lived in an imposing fifteen-room house fronted by four white pillars. She dragged me through a gleaming entrance hall into a salon that seemed to stretch for ever. Her mother, impeccably dressed and coiffed, sat at a gleaming desk writing on blue notepaper.

"This is Daryl!" Judy gushed.

Her mother eyed me sceptically. "Oh?" she said. She resembled her daughter, but was a more polished version in a tailored blue dress with an elegant gold pin perched on her shoulder. Judy, however, wore her favourite, tight black leather slacks and a peach angora sweater, the one that always shed its hairs on my jacket.

Her mother regarded us a moment. I think I half expected her to ask if we had an appointment. "Well, bye!" Judy said, dragging me along behind her.

When we pulled in my driveway, Judy said, "Wow! It's such a cute little house!"

In the university setting where I had met Judy, she seemed like so many other girls. She was buxom and hippy, a Rubens sort of girl, and her loudness and excessive vitality seemed natural in the frenzied world of all-night beer parties. But she was all, all wrong for our "cute little house" and – I anticipated – my cute little parents.

When Judy learned that they were not yet home, she said, "Oh, you devil!" and flung her arms around my neck and blew into my ear. I hate girls blowing into my ear. Unfortunately, this was one of Judy's favourite things to do. I expect she deemed it quite sexy.

I decided to show her the house, what little there was to show. "Isn't this *adorable*?" she said, and "How *quaint*!" and "You actually *live* here?"

"You probably don't want to see the upstairs—"

"Oh, I *do*!"

I should have known I was in trouble.

In my bedroom, she squealed. "It's so – *you*!" she said. She examined the bookshelf, my desk, the pictures on my wall. She lifted *The Tempest* from the nightstand. "*The Tempest*? Oh my, how very literary!" Then she drew her sweater up over her head and tossed the pile of angora fluff onto my bed. I had ogled this black lace brassière before, the one with wire hoops that uplifted her bulging breasts. When she unhooked the brassière, her breasts would fall. I always disliked that moment.

"Judy, I don't think—"

She unbuckled my belt.

"My parents will be—" I felt foolish protesting, for surely this was the girl's line, but the absolutely last place I wanted to bed a girl down was in my own house, and the absolutely last people I wanted to be discovered by were my own parents.

"Oh, you *silly*!" she said. She pressed herself against me and blew into my ear.

The doorbell rang.

"Oh, just for*get* the door!"

"Get dressed," I said, and fled, like a coward, down the stairs, tucking in my shirt, rebuckling my belt.

It was Nickel. I expected to see Mick hovering behind her, but she was alone. I let her in.

"I just wanted to see you," she said.

"Oh."

"Isn't anyone home?" she said, looking around.

"Well—"

"Could I talk to you?" She looked like an angel from God.

Judy came down the stairs, reclothed, brushing her hair with my hairbrush. I loathe it when anyone uses my hairbrush.

"Oh, *hi*!" Judy said. "Who's *this*, Daryl?" She pitched the hairbrush onto a chair, sidled up next to me and seized my arm.

Shrugging her loose, I moved away. I introduced them, miserable and dejected.

"Nickel? What a funny name!"

Nickel's gaze was even, steady. "I didn't know you were – I'll talk to you some other time," she said, drifting to the door.

I followed Nickel; Judy trailed me.

Jenny's car careened into the driveway. She looked in a foul mood, breezing past us on the steps, uttering only "Where's Mom?"

"Hello," Nickel offered. I wondered if Nickel called Jenny "Mrs Branch" now that Jenny was her teacher.

Jenny eyed her and said dismissively, "Nickel." Then she caught sight of Judy, glared back at me and at Nickel and said, "You having a party or what?" and went inside.

"It's OK," Nickel said to me, and left.

My parents returned.

"Oh, *hi*!" Judy said when introduced, and then, "You're looking so *well*!" which was, I thought, rather an odd thing for her to say, since she had never met them before.

My father, surprisingly, proffered a broad smile, and my mother was on the verge of returning Judy's gushes when she was interrupted by Jenny, who pulled her into the kitchen saying, "I need to talk with you!" Judy and I were left with my father. We sat on the sofa, facing his favourite chair. I saw him eye a half-full bowl of popcorn on the table, but he restrained himself and did not throw any out the window.

"So! Daryl's *father*!"

"Yes." I had expected him to brood, but he was almost animated. I had not seen his face rearrange itself into so many pleasing expressions in a long time. He seemed bemused.

"I guess you know him even better than *I*!" She gave me a seductive look.

"Maybe not." Somehow he seemed to know that this girl wore black brassières and that I had seen them.

"I *love* your house!"

"Ah," he said, glancing around the room.

41

I should have aided her, I should have contributed to the conversation, but I was paralysed with misery. Instead, I escaped to the kitchen on the pretext of getting us something to drink. My mother and Jenny were seated at the table. Jenny was pouring out a tale of woe; my mother was nodding.

"And all I was doing was tutoring—"

"Uh-huh."

"You'd think he'd appreciate the extra money—"

"Uh-huh."

"Maple is so selfish!"

"Uh-huh."

"He didn't even give Mick a chance to explain. He just said—"

I was not in the mood for hearing Jenny's latest tale; she was always running to my mother for solace, claiming Maple was selfish or that he did not understand her or that he did not pay attention to her, on and on she would go. Yet the next time I would see them together, they would be amorous, Jenny coquettish and wiggling as usual.

"We're leaving," I said.

"But Daryl—"

"We have to leave—"

"But, Daryl – I'm making fried chicken—"

"She has to—"

"But Daryl—"

Judy and I left. We had a pizza, saw a movie, parked on a country lane, her breasts fell, she blew in my ear, and on and on.

Eight

In previous years, I had visited the Malley house freely, but always in search of Joey or Danny Jr. Now, besotted with Nickel, I felt I had to contrive some intricate ruse in order to see her. For some reason, it seemed imperative that I not appear over-zealous nor expose my true intentions. Ah, had I only done so then.

Three weeks prior to this Christmas holiday, I had been awarded a role in the university's spring play, Shakespeare's *Tempest*. Auditioning was a lark; I very nearly did not attend, and I did not really expect to obtain a part. Too many other experienced drama students were vying for roles. The director said, later, that he had been seeking a "certain sort of innocence", and that is why he selected me. My ego deflated; innocence was not what I was attempting to project.

I admit to being disappointed when I first scanned the final cast list. Prince Ferdinand. It was a minor role; the character seemed almost simple-minded to me, *too* innocent and compliant. I think my brash ego had been hoping for – if any part – then the quintessential role: Prospero, that complex, formidable magician who can, at his command, open graves and wake their sleepers, create swirling tempests, torment his enemies, wreak vengeance, propel people about at will, and still be capable of forgiveness, still able to emerge humble and human as he posits himself in the power of his audience's imagination at the end of the play. But, Ferdinand I was given, and Ferdinand I would be. We had been in the early stage of rehearsals when school broke up for the December vacation, but we were admonished to be off-book by our return in January.

When I returned from my fiasco excursion with Judy, I lay on my bed, still despondent and agitated, not entirely sure why. My copy of *The Tempest* lay on the nightstand. As I flipped through it, I hit upon an idea: I could ask Nickel to cue me – a magnificent excuse to be with her, I thought. It now seems enormously banal and transparent.

Nonetheless, the following day, I went to the Malleys with the book in my jacket pocket, in search of Nickel, little aware of the tempest brewing within the Malley household.

After knocking, I thought I heard muffled shouting inside. Although I was not able to decipher exact words, I was fairly certain it was Dan's booming voice and Imogen's whine that I could hear. I stepped back, debating whether to leave or persist. I had never heard them argue. A door slammed, more shouting, and then I thought I heard Nickel wail. I pounded on the door.

Suddenly, all was quiet. Through the portières I could see someone coming downstairs. Dan Malley opened the door. His face was reddened, and he was breathing heavily. For a moment, I thought I recognized the look on his face; it was the glare I had seen when he stepped into the tent that time that in all innocence I had crawled in with Nickel to escape a wet sleeping bag. He quickly composed himself, however, and asked me in, all the while apologizing that Joey wouldn't be home until next week and Danny was finishing his painting of the school. I expected that he would lead me into the kitchen where Imogen would join us and offer something to eat and drink, as usual, but we remained standing in the entrance hallway.

"You could go on up to the school," Dan offered.

"Well—"

"It's OK–although Danny will probably get you to help him with the painting!"

44

"Well—"

"Go on, he'll be glad to see you."

Behind him, Imogen slowly descended the stairs. She stopped before she reached the bottom and said, "Oh. Daryl." She avoided looking me in the eye, her face slightly averted.

Mustering up what little boldness remained, I asked if Nickel was home.

"No," Dan said quickly, "no, she is not at home."

When Imogen turned her head sharply to stare at Dan, I noticed that one side of her face was discoloured.

Dan must have realized how abrupt he had sounded for he added, "She's probably off with that goddam Mick!" He attempted a laugh.

It was obvious that I was not welcome, so I turned to leave. Oddly, Dan Malley put his hand on my shoulder and said, "How is Jenny?" I replied that she was fine, and I left, in search of Danny. On the way, my mind ran riot. I imagined that Nickel was imprisoned in her room and Dan had taken to beating both his daughter and his wife, and that I could have rescued the two women if I had been more courageous. Later, I thought that Shakespeare's tempestuous world must have been too much with me, accounting for my vision of heroes and villains, beautiful heroines and bestial Calibans.

But I had not erred entirely in my assumptions.

It had been several years since I was last inside Burton High School and it seemed to have diminished in size: the halls had surely contracted, the ceilings had been lowered. The smell, however, was the same: that mixed concoction of floor wax, dirty gym clothes, hamburger grease, after-shave and perfume.

I sought out my old locker, 62-B, the focal point of all that social manoeuvring that was characteristic of adolescence. Between-class and after-school visits to the locker offered chance meetings with friends, with girls, with strangers who might enter one's life at any moment and alter it for ever.

I could remember dawdling there, with the locker door flung open, aimlessly sifting through papers and books and gym clothes, squandering time, socializing.

"Who are you taking to the dance?"

"Me? Oh, I don't know."

"How about Sally? She's got the hots for you!" Leer, leer.

"Naw – how do you know, anyway?"

Leer, leer. "I heard her tell Mary in Chem. class—"

"Naw – I hardly know her."

"What the hell – take a chance!"

"Well—"

"There she is."

"Well—"

"Go on, you coward."

"Hi."

"Hi there."

"I'm Daryl."

"I know."

"You're Sally?"

"Uh-hmm."

"Well."

"Well what?"

"You going to the dance on Saturday?"

"I don't know yet."

"Oh."

"Mmm. Are you?"

"Going to the dance? Oh, well, I don't know yet."

"Oh."

Long, boundless, interminable pause.

"Would you like to go?"

"Me? What, with you?"

"Well, yes."

"Oh."

"Well, if you have other plans—"

"Like I said, I'm not sure yet—"

"Oh."

Oh, the pain of it all.

I found Danny in the hallway leading to the art rooms. One side of this hallway was flanked with lockers. On the upper half of the other side hung a long uninterrupted stretch of bulletin boards displaying student art work; the lower half of this wall was a clean expanse of white paint, except, that is, for the section Danny was working on. He was slapping white paint over a colourful mural that still stretched another four or five feet in width beyond what he had already covered.

Danny was at that age where he seemed to grow taller before your eyes; surely he was a good six inches taller than when I had seen him a few months ago. He wore blue jeans and a black T-shirt with a bright red sun on the back and seemed all arms, legs, hands and feet as I approached him. But although he appeared gangly at first sight, he was muscular and solid: bulging biceps, sturdy legs, a thick, strong neck. Danny's head did not seem to have kept up with the growth of the rest of his body, for it looked oddly small and pixie-ish resting on that sturdy neck.

He turned when I called his name. His face was lean and his eyes rested in deep hollows. His look, at first defiant, quickly changed to relief, and then to one of shared camaraderie. I expected him to tempt me to deface the walls he had so recently recovered.

I stood back to admire what remained of his mural. Bright strokes of red, black, white, blue and gold paint delineated contorted figures on galloping steeds, shining

47

swords, bolts of lightning, one figure thrusting a sickle into the ground, another treading enormous grapes bursting blood-red splashes into the air and onto the horses' necks. Beyond this, a ball of fire erupted from the centre of a smooth lake; a white-cloaked figure girdled in gold stood at the edge, holding aloft what appeared to be a test tube filled with blood.

"It's called 'Apocalypse'," he said.

What struck me was the suppressed violence of the painting, but Danny was obviously talented. It was skilfully executed, its strokes bold and sure, its proportions exaggerated but effective, its composition intricately balanced.

"God!" I said.

"Well, I didn't get God in there yet—"

"No, I meant, god what an amazing painting!"

"Yeah, well Old Hairy doesn't think so."

"Old Hairy" was the students' irreverent nickname for Mr Lawrence Upton, the principal.

"No?"

"He said I should have asked *permission* and that if everyone went around painting whatever he wanted all over the walls – et cetera – you can imagine what he said." Danny assumed Mr Upton's characteristic stance and, mimicking Mr Upton's voice, said: "Besides, it's too violent! It is not appropriate viewing material for impressionable adolescents!" Danny shrugged. "My art teacher liked it though. Still, he won't fight Old Hairy. So I have to cover up my masterpiece. Want to help?" He held out his brush. "There's another brush here somewhere—"

We spent the next few hours cloaking Danny's portentous vision. Danny rambled on about painting. He was obviously obsessed with it, finding in it an outlet for all those "different beats" he heard and also reaping from it some measure of acceptance and recognition, as well as a new persona – that of the artistic rebel.

I was intrigued by what he had to say, and so much of what he said I found myself applying to Prospero, for both Danny and Prospero were obsessed with the power of creating visible replications of their extraordinary imaginations. Again I regretted being merely the rather banal Prince Ferdinand.

But what I remember most about that day I helped Danny repaint the hallway was that each of us released a secret.

As I was effacing the test tube of blood (Danny said it was a "vial filled with wrath"), I blurted, "I think I'm in love with Nickel."

Danny's response startled me. "Isn't everyone?"

I do not know what I expected. Perhaps I thought he would embrace me, wish me luck, divulge that Nickel harboured the same feelings for me. Who knows what I hoped for; I was so pathetic, it seems in retrospect, so entranced, so desperate.

"No, I mean I am *really* in love with her," I said.

"I heard you. And I said, 'Isn't *everyone*?' Sorry, Daryl, but I hear it all the time. All-the-time. Guys come up to me every single day and want me to introduce them to her and want to know where she lives and who she likes and if she and Mick are going to last and—"

"Are they?"

"Nickel and Mick? Who knows. The trouble with Nickel is that she loves everybody just the same. She has an enormous capacity for that. It's just that Mick is obsessed; he won't give up."

"So she's just putting up with him? She can't get rid of him?" I was momentarily encouraged.

"She loves him OK, just like everyone else though."

"Oh."

"Don't look so damn depressed, Daryl. I'll tell you something. I've never told anybody else. I love Nickel too."

This surprised me only because I surely did not feel this way about my own sister. "So?" I said.

"No, I mean I *really* love her. Like you do."

"God!" The thought repelled me.

"The problem with growing up with someone like Nickel is that other girls seem petty and shallow in comparison. Quit looking so disgusted. So I'm a pervert. Big deal."

"I didn't say you were a pervert."

"Yeah, but you're thinking it. Don't worry, I'd never touch her."

"Jesus." And just before I swept my brush across the face of the girdled angel, I realized that it was Nickel's face in profile that Danny had painted. You couldn't mistake it.

Nine

A more tenacious person might have doubled his pursuit of Nickel, regardless of – even spurred onward by – the apparently overwhelming competition. I, however, was at least temporarily deterred and spent the rest of the vacation wallowing in self-pity, but instead of scorning this object of my unrequited love, I indulged myself in further embellishing my already elaborately drawn portrait of the one and only Nickel Malley. At least in my imagination she was mine.

I suppose I should have realized how dangerously

powerful she was becoming through these waking dreams. Unaware that I was taking on the attributes of the white knight, I championed her at every turn, much to the dismay of both Dan Malley and my sister Jenny.

I had abandoned the idea of asking Nickel to cue me for my lines in *The Tempest* and I had forsworn making any further approaches for the time being. The monastic exercise of isolating myself in my room, reciting Ferdinand's lines over and over, became a sort of calming ritual. Then Jenny visited one day and offered to "test" my progress. I agreed, somewhat reluctantly, recalling all too clearly previous aborted tutorial sessions with her.

The "rehearsal" went surprisingly well at first. She even seemed impressed at my command of Ferdinand's lines and did not mock my interpretation – not, that is, until the third act when Ferdinand and the beautiful Miranda are alone.

Jenny cued, "Do you love me?"

And I, with perhaps too much passion, replied, "O heaven! O earth!" Before I could continue, however, Jenny was sniggering and pretending to fall off the chair.

"God!" she said. "What a fool!"

"What?" I was deeply offended and embarrassed.

"This Miranda character. 'Do you love me?' She's only just met the guy! And *you*. 'O heaven! O earth!'" She was laughing herself half to death.

"Get on with it," I said.

We managed a few more lines, but I could see Jenny beginning to erupt again as she cued, "My husband then?"

And passionately, I answered, "Ay, with a heart as willing/As bondage e'er of freedom: here's my hand."

"Oh God!" Jenny said, scornfully.

And then I made my blunder. I said, "Will you just get *on* with it. Read Nickel's line."

"*What*? Read *whose* line? Read *Nickel's* line? Oh my, oh my, how very Freudian, Daryl! So, you've given yourself away! You ass."

I was mortified. Had I really used Nickel's name in place of Miranda's? I made a pitiful attempt to shrug off my error, but Jenny was not deterred.

"I'm surprised at you, Daryl. If you're going to pick someone to worship, why don't you at least pick someone *worthy* of it? Why don't you at least pick somebody *human*?"

I did not want to get drawn into this battle. It was not easy to win with Jenny, who locks on to her prey with steel talons, but she persisted in pecking away at my most vulnerable spots. "What about that red-headed what's-her-name you brought home? Isn't she more your type? Wouldn't you rather have someone you can hop into the sack with than—"

I snatched the book from Jenny. "Forget it," I said. "Just forget it."

Dan Malley strolled up the back walk, carrying a Christmas tin.

"Imogen wanted me to bring this over," he said. "It's a fruit cake."

A friend of mine has a theory that there are only five fruit cakes in the world and that people keep passing them on to others, that no one ever actually eats one.

"Hello, Dan." With one hand, Jenny reached back and lifted her long hair off her neck, shaking it loose. Then she slid her hand inside her blouse and adjusted a strap.

"The lovely Jenny," he said, leaning over to kiss her cheek. "I can see down your shirt."

"Ha ha."

Turning to me, Dan asked, "Did you ever find Danny?"

"Yes, at the school."

"God!" Jenny said. "Did he get that mural off the wall? I don't know, Dan, your kids are so much trouble!"

"Except for Nickel," he said.

"The perfect Nickel. By the way," she said, and I knew immediately from the tone of her voice that she would expose me, "Daryl here seems to have fallen under Nickel's spells along with the multitudes."

I wanted to lean over and put my hands around her throat and squeeze until that sharp tongue was silenced. I stared at her, but she had turned to look at Dan and had such a curious expression on her face that I followed her gaze. Dan's upper lip was raised, like a dog preparing to defend his territory. But once again, he quickly recovered, and mocked his own reaction.

"Watch it, Daryl," he said, with feigned ferocity.

"Don't believe everything you hear," I said. "Jenny has a great imagination."

"Oh my poor Daryl," she said, "you really are a goner."

Mustering all my maturity, I responded as I have always responded when I get cornered: I left the room. I offered a thin excuse, something about having to memorize my lines. Once in my bedroom, I indulged in equally mature actions. I slammed the door, I kicked my wastebasket, I threw the book at the wall, and all the while I was keenly aware of my puerile attempts to assuage my frustration. I was nearly twenty years old. What, I wondered, would a real hero have done?

Although Jenny is now a mother herself and transformed for ever as a result, in that year leading up to Dan's death maternity seemed the furthest thing from her mind.

53

And it was, perhaps, after all, although few would like to think that her beautiful Andrea was one of those unbidden accidents of nature, brought into this world to teach us all a lesson.

My mother said, at Andrea's birth, "Big vessel is made slowly."

Just prior to my return to school after that Christmas holiday, I saw Jenny getting into her car in a department-store parking lot. I called to her, and she whirled around. "Oh!" she said. "You frightened me, Daryl." Her face was flushed, her hair uncharacteristically mussed. "I was just getting some things," she said.

"I'm off tomorrow, back to school."

"Oh. Well, then. Good luck, or rather 'break a leg'! Maybe I'll come and see you in the play – when is it?"

Surprised by her interest, I gave her the dates and mentioned which day our parents planned to attend. "Come along," I said.

"Well, I might, but maybe on my own."

The notion that Jenny would drive a hundred and fifty miles to glimpse me in a school play was nothing short of astounding. "Don't expect too much," I said.

Then, on the other side of the parking lot, near the entrance, a car nearly backed into me. "Hey!" I thumped the rear fender. The driver, a young boy, turned around. "You nearly hit me," I said, and then I saw that it was Mick.

My impulse was to berate him – not for nearly hitting me, but for his place in Nickel's heart. He appeared shaken though, by the near miss, and I merely said, "Forget it," and strode away in my best imitation of an older college student.

At school, I became entrenched in play rehearsals and weekend partying, and had little time to dwell on life back in Burton. I did still dream of Nickel and kept a picture of her on my bureau, but I was currently being pursued by Rita, the blonde Miranda playing opposite me. Perhaps, because I delivered my lines to an imaginary Nickel, I conveyed too much passion in rehearsals, or maybe it is typical for dramatic romances to be re-enacted outside the theatre, but Rita had obviously decided I was a true prince. It flattered my ego at a time when it needed it, I suppose. Our relationship built swiftly enough that after the dress rehearsal, one day before opening, she revealed her other charms to me. It was a relief, I think, to see a pink brassière for a change.

We played our parts well, each convincing in our eagerness for the other, each rather over-brimming with ardour. My parents attended the second performance and, with Rita clinging to my arm, my mother told me I was "brilliant" and "handsome". My father said, "Not bad," but he looked tired. I asked if they were spending the night at a motel, hoping that they were not, as I wanted to celebrate with Rita, and thankfully my mother said, "Oh, no. Barney likes to sleep in his own bed, don't you, Barney?"

"Yup."

Two nights later, on Saturday, I was still changing out of my costume when Jenny rushed backstage.

"Oh! Sorry! Don't worry," she said to the underwear-clad Prospero. "I've seen it all before!"

"Jenny?"

"Daryl, you were quite convincing!"

"Why didn't you tell me you were coming?"

"Well, I told you I might—"

"Where's Maple?"

"Oh, I didn't come with Maple. Are you kidding? Shakespeare? No, I came on my own—"

"Just to see me?"

"Don't sound so surprised!"

Rita came to the doorway. "Everybody decent?" she called. "Daryl?"

Jenny appraised her carefully. "The lovely Miranda," she said to me. "Well, that's more like it anyway!" She left soon after, and again I was grateful that she didn't expect me to entertain her, for Rita's roommate was away for the weekend and the cast was going to celebrate.

That night, at Rita's apartment, after the guests had left, I detected the telling signs of a dwindling infatuation. Jenny's "approval" of Rita had been gnawing at me, and I found myself thinking of Nickel most of the evening. When Rita blew softly into my ear and said, "What shall we do tomorrow?" I knew I would be on the run again.

That "insubstantial pageant" had faded, although the groundwork had all been laid for the next big drama of my life, one that was to be played to a less appreciative audience.

Ten

Like most families, ours possesses its hoard of tales, vignettes that, increasingly, my mother delights in reviving, despite her repeated admonishment that "Life's a book, you can't go turning back those pages". She recounts one about me that I have been musing over lately. Her version goes something like this.

She will tell me I was "no saint" and "a real trial". She will assert that I would defy anyone if I wanted to find out something. Then she will ask if I remember that day when I was five years old and we were in the kitchen, with the door open, one of those hot, steamy summer days. A thunderstorm was blowing in. We were watching it, she will say.

Next she will tell me that I was standing in the doorway, and she was at the sink "trying to hurry up and finish those dishes in case lightning struck the water supply and zapped into the faucet" and killed her. She will remind me of the metal strip around the door frame and across the doorstep, and she will remind me that she said, "Daryl, you step back, don't let your foot touch that metal in case lightning hits."

She will recount that I pulled my foot back, and she turned to the dishes again. She does not know what made her turn back around, but she did. She will repeat this: "There you were, slowly inching your little foot back onto that metal strip with this sneaky grin on your face. Lord. What a trial."

Oddly, I can summon this moment as clearly as she can, although I do not recall any awareness of intentional defiance. What clings with me is the incredible surge of excitement I felt as my foot moved back onto that metal strip. To be able to *feel* lightning, to think that in an instant all might change, be illuminated, be known and felt – that's what I remember. That it might kill me in the process was incomprehensible.

It is this sort of penchant for potential excitement and an inability to perceive its incumbent dangers that led me into the Dan Malley turmoil, I think.

The "dress rehearsal" for the event took place shortly over a year after my Prince Ferdinand debut. It was March, the snows had melted, crocuses were blooming all over campus, daffodils were promising to bloom, and I

57

was a junior in college, abruptly aware that not only were the deadlines for two long-term papers converging with menacing rapidity, but also that I was alarmingly close to being thrust out into the "real" world with absolutely no notion of what I might do then.

I sought refuge at home one weekend, telling myself that I would be free of distractions and thus able to complete the two papers. What a mistake.

When I arrived home late Friday afternoon, Wilma Taylor, a neighbour, was sitting in the kitchen with my mother. They fussed over me, as usual, insisting I join them and recount my latest adventures. I should have foreseen that with Wilma present, only she would be relating adventures, but once I sat down I was snared.

Wilma was known for several things: her loquacity, her vanity, her hats and her obsession with tales of disaster. On this day, she wore a navy blue dress with a pink collar and matching pink belt, navy blue shoes, and on her head, a navy blue hat with pink and white flowers fastened to its navy blue ribbon. She wore thick make-up, her eyelashes heavily coated, her cheeks overly pink and her lips brilliant red. On a spare chair rested her navy blue coat and a pair of navy blue cloth gloves.

My mother tells a tale about Wilma's hats, that is not so much a story of Wilma but of my mother. I had heard her recount this story many times and thus should have learned something from it, but I had not.

My mother had always considered Wilma Taylor to be "Miss Vanity Personified", and evidence of this was seen in Wilma's collection of hats: hats of every colour, material and shape, hats to match every outfit, hats with feathers, with flowers, with netting, with fruit and nuts. People, my mother included, gossiped about Wilma's vanity: "Did you *see* what she has on *today*?" and "Who does she think she *is*?" and "She looks like a little *partridge*!" and on and on.

But, one day in Beegray's Department Store, my mother spied an irresistible hat: pale blue velvet covered in blue netting, with sprigs of lavender tucked into the hatband beside a blue rose. She will say that it seemed to have her name written on the tag: "Sairy Wilson, come and get me." And she will recall that the saleswoman assured her she looked so *young* and so *pretty* in it, and she will acknowledge that the saleswoman would have said those things even if my mother had placed a trash bag on her head, but she bought it anyway, because *she* liked it.

She knew that it was a foolish purchase; the only place she could wear it was to church ("A hat is a little protection from too much God"), and, feeling a bit guilty, she manufactured excuses for buying it. She told Imogen that her other hat was "worn all to pieces"; she told my father that she thought her "head was getting bigger – my other hat's too tight". At home, in the privacy of the bathroom, she tried it on at least a hundred times that first week. She admired it from every angle. It was a wonderful hat.

That Sunday, she wore it to church, feeling transformed, feigning shyness and diffidence in the face of her friends' compliments. "Oh this?" she said. "This little thing? Do you really like it?"

She and my father sat in the tenth pew, where they always sat, but soon she heard whispering, and she turned just as Wilma Taylor entered the church in a "silly blue dress and some silly hat perched on her head with little bits of grass sticking out the top". Then my mother noticed Imogen a few rows back, with her mouth open, staring from my mother to Wilma and back again, and sure enough, Wilma and my mother were wearing identical hats.

In the retelling of this story, my mother will, at this moment, emit a long sigh, pregnant with humility. She will swear that at that moment, she had "a little vision" in which she realized that "everybody's just the same", and this vision expanded, next revealing to her that "there are no saints and there are no villains". Another long sigh will follow. Then she will say that she was momentarily elated. She realized that "I'm just as good as anybody else – no one is better than me". But almost immediately, she became depressed. No one, she thought, is any worse than me either. With one final sigh, she will offer her final understanding of this lesson: "There's just a long line of people beating their paths through the jungle any which way they can."

If I could only have absorbed this much, much earlier, I might have avoided taking a role in a drama which I did not understand.

And although I can hardly lay the blame on Wilma Taylor, it may have been her tales of destructive passion on that Friday afternoon that helped distort my vision.

I am not sure what precipitated this story, not that Wilma needed any reasonable excuse to relate one of her tales, but something prompted her to say, "Sairy, you just can't believe what people do when they are driven by desire."

"Oh?" My mother understood that Wilma liked to be led on, encouraged.

"There was this woman, see? Everybody thought she was a normal person, see? People thought she was attractive – although in the magazine picture, you could see she was a little plump—"

Wilma prides herself on remaining trim.

"—and she has this husband, see? Everybody thought they were a normal couple—"

"Who's *everybody*?" I asked. It was a mistake.

Wilma looked annoyed. She sniffed. "Honestly, Daryl, all the people that the magazine *interviewed*—"

My mother shot me a knowing glance.

"Ah," I said, "*everybody*."

Wilma did not miss a beat. "Anyway, this lady got some notion in her head that she was going to die. Everybody said that was just craziness on her part. And she started worrying that she would die and her husband would marry someone else and—"

"How did they know?" I asked.

"Know *what*?"

"Know that she was worrying that she would die and—"

"Honestly, Daryl. I don't remember. It's all in the magazine. Do you want to hear this or not?" She fiddled with her pink collar.

"Of course we do, Wilma," my mother said. "Daryl, be quiet."

"Well, this lady was *so* worried that her husband would up and marry some young pretty slip of a girl that she put poison in his coffee—"

My mother glanced down at her coffee cup.

"What kind of poison?"

"Daryl!"

"Oh, sorry."

"And when he was dead in her bed," Wilma relished this part, you could tell, because she leaned over, first to my mother and then to me, so close that I could smell the newness of her hat, "she put him in the *freezer*!"

"The *freezer*?"

Wilma seized my mother's arm. "The *deep* freeze! The way she got caught was that she went to a taxidermist! She wanted to know if he could stuff a *person*!"

"The taxidermist turned her in?"

"Whose story *is* this, Daryl? Did you read the article? No, you didn't. It is not important how or if she got caught. Now, when the taxidermist man came to the house and she showed him the body in the freezer, all she could say was how much she loved her husband and how she wanted him with her – stuffed, of course – till she died and then they could be buried together."

"My."

"Go ahead, don't believe it, but it's *true*. It was in the *magazine*. You just can't know what people will do in the name of love. It's passion, pure passion."

"Sounds like jealousy to me," I ventured.

"Same thing," Wilma said, "same thing."

What puzzles me is that I could detect the relationship between jealousy and passion so easily, so quickly, in Wilma's story, but not in the "story" brewing on our own street.

Wilma had many more tales like that. She had heard about men who tied women up and hid them in closets so they would not flirt with other men, and about men with fifty wives, and about women who chopped off their husband's ears or genitals (Wilma called them "gentles") for love tokens, or people who kept their dead spouse in the house, all "smelly and rotten", and on and on. She savoured these stories.

My father would not come anywhere near when Wilma was playing bard. "Chatterbox," he would say. If he had had occasion to relate any of her tales, he would not have become involved in *why* the woman did it or what kind of poison; he would have seen no need to draw out the story.

My mother was as easily frustrated with my father's stories, however. "You leave too much out," she would say. "You tell a story and then I go outside and I'm pulling up weeds an hour later and I wonder now why did she do that and what did he say and so on. Nothing's black or white. Nothing's even grey. It's all shades of the rainbow and you can't describe a rainbow without mentioning all the colours and the sky behind and the mist and all that goes with it, can you? And besides, Barney," she would add, "you ought to use some verbs."

And how, I find myself wondering, would my father have recounted the story of Dan Malley, the story of Nickel, the story of Mick, of all of us who were "principals" in that drama? Surely, he would condense it all, but my version will be more like Wilma's than my father's; I will have to include all the colours of the rainbow.

Eleven

I awakened the next morning to the sound of Jenny's shouting in the kitchen, directly below my room. When I joined the fracas, she was pacing back and forth, opening and slamming drawers at random.

"He is *so* insensitive. Honest to God."

"Now, Jenny—" My mother was washing the dishes.

"He won't even let Mick—"

"The bumblebee boy? Hi, Jenny—"

"Oh shut *up*, Daryl."

"Jenny!"

"Hello, Daryl. How nice to see you. I am not in a very good mood right now. I am about to kill my husband."

"Now, Jenny—"

"So he comes in and there's Mick sitting at the table. I swear to God, all I was doing was helping him with an essay—"

"You still teach him? Did he fail English last year?"

"Oh, for God's sake, Daryl. No, he did not fail English last year. He's only the most brilliant student I have ever taught—"

"Then why does he need help on his paper?"

"Christ! You sound just like Maple!"

"Well," my mother said, "it's a reasonable question, Jenny."

"It's a goddam *college* admissions essay, that's why. He wants it to be *perfect*, that's why. What is this, an inquisition?"

My mother placed two grapefruit halves on the table. "You kids sit down and eat some grapefruit," she said.

"Christ! I don't want to eat any damn *grapefruit*!"

"Jenny, your language is getting out of hand."

"God!" But she did sit down and she did begin to pick at the grapefruit.

"Hi, Daryl," I said to myself, "how are you? How is school? What are you doing home? How have you been?"

"Ha, ha."

"Why," my mother asked, "don't you tutor Mick up at the school?"

"Be*cause* we talk about other things too. There's no privacy at school."

"No *privacy*?"

"God, Daryl. Mick has some problems. You should hear about his family. His father's drunk half the time. He's never home. All his mother talks about is the damn library. And he's got problems with Nickel—"

"Oh?" I asked.

"Oh, wouldn't you like to know about Mick and Nickel! Are you still in *love* with her, Daryl?"

My mother said, "What? What's this? Daryl?"

"Forget it," I said. "She's imagining things again."

"Right. You could care less. Well, too bad, because poor Mick is even more besotted than you are and the Queen of Sheba barely knows he's alive."

"Oh?"

"But you know what he told me today? This is rather strange. He said Dan Malley bought a gun."

"Whatever for?" I asked.

"Well, the Taylors did get broken into," my mother said, "when they were at church. They were only gone an hour, and when they returned, everything was in total disarray! They stole Wilma's jewellery and some of her hats—"

"Oh, come on!" Jenny said. "Who would want to steal her old hats?"

"I surely do not know, but she's all upset. They stole her mink hat and I don't remember which other ones, but maybe—"

"So you think Dan bought a gun because the Taylors' house was broken into?" I asked.

"Well, probably. I don't believe in having guns, but what would I do if someone broke in here with Barney the way he is? Oh my."

"I don't think that's why Dan bought the gun," Jenny said. "Mick is afraid. He thinks Dan is going to kill him."

"Jenny!" my mother said.

"You're kidding," I said. "That's ridiculous."

"Oh?" she said. "Well, Mick is convinced."

"Jenny Wilson Branch, you stop that. That's a terrible thing to say about Dan Malley. Why would he want to kill Mick? He's such a nice boy. Nice people like

Dan Malley don't go around shooting nice boys like Mick."

"Well, *you* believe that and *I* believe that, but Mick thinks that Dan doesn't like all the time Mick spends with Nickel and that Dan suspects that he and Nickel are shacking up—"

"Jenny!"

"I didn't say they *were* shacking up—"

"Jenny!"

"—but that's what Mick thinks that Dan thinks."

"Huh?"

"*I* know they're not shacking up—"

"Jenny!"

"And how do you know that?" I asked.

Jenny actually blushed, which surprised me, because this was just the sort of talk that she relished. "I just know," she said. "Besides – the Queen of Sheba? Shacking up?"

"Jenny Wilson Branch!"

"God, Mother, don't sound so *naïve*."

My mother was not the only one who was naïve.

I had not seen Nickel in a long time. My life no longer revolved entirely around the Malleys, although it may seem so in this recollection. I had spent the previous summer completing an internship at school, returning home at least half a dozen weekends in the past year, but I had only seen Nickel twice – and on the same day.

In the morning of that day, I visited the Malleys, and Nickel was with Mick. Again she said, "I wish we could talk," and there seemed something urgent in her manner, but we could not free ourselves of Mick. She came to my house later that day and we set out for a walk.

It was exhilarating to walk down the street with Nickel. It was a brilliant late summer's day. She wore white shorts and a red T-shirt, her legs and arms were very brown, her hair was shiny, her skin glowed, she smelled of jasmine. It is impossible to talk of her without clichés. Alas. But I thought, that day, this is what it could be like: Nickel and I strolling along, talking; the world a magnificent place.

She said, "I don't ever get to see you any more."

"You always have company."

"And you're always at school."

Nickel is an affectionate person, given to gently touching people as she talks. She will lay her hand on your arm or against your ribs or on your shoulder, softly and freely and innocently. We rounded the corner of our street, she had just placed her hand on my shoulder, and the sun glinting off the street made it seem paved with silver. It was a splendid, dazzling moment. And there, loping toward us, was Mick.

"Oh," Nickel said, her voice betraying neither disappointment nor excitement.

Mick stopped, and we approached him.

"Mick, you've met Daryl, haven't you?"

"We're just out for a walk," I said stupidly, willing myself to be assertive, intending to hold my ground and my right to walk with Nickel.

"Where to?" he said.

"Oh, just around."

"Around where?"

I looked at Nickel; she looked at me. "Where were we going?" I asked.

She shrugged. "Nowhere. Nowhere, really."

"Let's go get a Coke then," he said.

The truth is, I could not bear it. I suggested they go on ahead, that maybe I would join them shortly, knowing that I would not, and I went home.

*

That was the only time I had seen Nickel in the past year. But after Jenny told us about the gun, I went over to the Malleys, sceptical, I suppose, but also curious.

Danny was in the back yard hurling a baseball against the garage.

"Been painting any more murals lately?" I asked.

"Yeah, come here." He led me around the side of the garage and showed me his most recent efforts. The painting covered the full side of the garage. A woman in a white hooded cloak stood in the centre, her face hidden by a black veil. In her hands, she cradled a basket of bright red apples. Surrounding her lurked sinister dark trees, their branches grotesquely bent and ending in finger-like projections which reached toward the woman.

"Snow White?" I said. "Garden of Eden?"

Danny laughed and laughed. Then he said, quite soberly, "Apocalypse Two."

From where we were standing, we could see straight down the driveway. Jenny's car pulled up, Dan stepped out, paused, and leaned back in the window. Jenny opened her door, and the two of them came down the driveway.

"Hello, Daryl," Dan said. "Admiring my son's latest masterpiece? Let me show you mine." He opened the garage door, and we followed him inside. On a shelf above the work bench sat a wooden box, which he withdrew. Inside was another box and inside that was a gleaming revolver. "Not bad, eh?"

Jenny stepped back. Danny apparently had seen it already, for he merely smiled.

"What's that for?" I asked.

"You never know," Dan said, "you never know." Then he elbowed my ribs and said, "Don't look so mortified. Lots of people have guns. I have a licence. I grew up with

68

guns, my dad showed me how to use one when I was ten years old."

"Yeah," Danny said, "but he only just showed me."

"Well, your mother wouldn't ever let me have one in the house when you kids were little. Suspicious, Imogen is."

"Or cautious," I said.

"I think that's horrible!" Jenny said. "Get rid of it."

Dan put his arm around her. "Now, now."

Mick's car pulled in the driveway, and he and Nickel got out. They stood for a moment, as if deciding whether or not to join us, and then Nickel walked into the garage with Mick just behind her.

"I'll have a little fun," Dan whispered to Jenny. Then he stepped toward Mick, aiming the gun at him. "Watch it, Mick," he said.

I have no recollection of what happened after Nickel screamed, but according to Jenny, I yanked Nickel back, out of the way, and both Mick and I lunged for the gun.

Apparently Dan dropped it and said, "Jesus, can't anyone take a joke?"

It was a lousy joke.

I also do not remember the argument that ensued. Mick apparently tried to persuade Nickel to leave with him, but Dan refused to let her go, and finally Jenny and Mick left.

The next thing I recall about that day is sitting in my bedroom, aimlessly drawing on a sheet of white paper. I still have the drawing. It is a replica of Danny's painting on the side of the Malleys' garage.

Although I was later gratified that my actions – protecting the damsel in distress – appeared almost heroic, I was shaken by the incident and by my inability to recall what I had done. All I could remember thinking was that it was not Mick that was going to be shot, but Nickel, and that somehow if Nickel were shot, something terrible would happen to me as well. It bothered me that I did not seem at all concerned for Mick's safety, since he was the one who was really being threatened – or so it seemed. I did not appreciate Dan Malley's joke, nor did I like the sinister, foreboding look on his face as he aimed the gun at Mick. I had to remind myself that he was only pretending.

Oddly, the scene resurrected a moment in our production of *The Tempest*, when Prospero approaches his malevolent brother. Our Prospero was built somewhat like Dan Malley and wore an improbable black wig, but could contort his face swiftly, moving from horrendous grimaces to benevolent smiles in an instant. Prospero, the great magician, the man capable of the "rarer act" of virtue and yet equally capable of manipulation, bondage and torture.

Twelve

Two months later, at school, I received an invitation to Nickel's graduation. Enclosed was a simple, sweet letter in which she said that she "sincerely hoped" I would attend, as it "would mean very much" to her. Do women presume that men don't make much of these things? Sometimes I think that we are guilty of more sentimentality and mawkishness than women are. My roommate once confessed that for seven years he had kept a note from "the girl back home". The note read, "Meet me at the corner at two o'clock."

In similar fashion, I folded Nickel's letter and concealed it in my wallet. Of course I would go, despite the ceremony's inconvenient date, barely a week before my final exams, and I would desperately need every available moment to study.

When Nickel's letter arrived, six weeks before the scheduled graduation, I was in the midst of rehearsals for yet another play, Miller's *Death of a Salesman*. I had been a little less diffident concerning try-outs, for this time I coveted a part, but I still aimed for a more substantial and salient role than the one I was awarded. I was to portray Happy, the profligate but lonely bachelor, the young man who never grew up, the sometimes fatuous, often star-gazing Happy Loman. The director said, "You're just the sort of boyish, dreamy young man who could pull this off." Boyish? Dreamy? These were not, I thought, flattering appellations.

I find it difficult to play a role if I do not like the character. I had been taught that an actor had to reach down inside himself and withdraw fragments of the character he was portraying. I wanted to pull out grand, flamboyant bits: righteous anger, noble disdain, sublime love. I knew that I would unearth pieces of Happy Loman in me, but I was not eager to devote two months delving for them and then flaunting them, bald and unarrayed, on stage.

Like Happy Loman, I fancied all those emblems of material success: the automobile, the apartment, the money. And I knew that, like Happy, I would probably learn, in fact already sensed, that they would not bring me happiness, such an elusive dream. Also resembling Happy, I yearned for the moon and the stars, but I expected them to cascade into my lap.

71

But I discovered, as well, other shocking similarities between me and Happy. He squandered girls as capriciously as I had, and I deemed him despicable for it. He treated his father like a worn rug, as I had, not so much overtly abusing, but merely indifferent and oblivious, and I condemned Happy for this. His face to the world was carefree, naïvely hopeful, and I had worn this visage too long to ignore the likeness. "*If only*," he would say, and I had thought this every day of my life – if only things would come my way, if only I had money, if only I could find the right pursuit, if only Mick would vanish, if only I had Nickel.

However, while I was able to reach down and identify these shards of Happy's character in me in order to be a better actor, I had not learned enough to alter my behaviour permanently. I was still capable of squandering girls and money, I was still guilty of ignoring my father, I was still going to expect the moon and stars and Nickel Malley to descend into my lap one day.

There was something disgustingly wicked in my growing relationship with the girl who played the part of Linda Loman, my mother, in this play. The actress, Rachel, did not resemble any of the other girls I had dated. She was thin and wiry, nervous and mercurial, plain and freckled. But she had piercing black eyes that would fasten on you with such intensity that you felt a bit dazed. You felt yourself being drawn in, slowly and purposefully. The actor who played the part of my brother had first noticed the unsettling effect of her gaze. He had been having particular difficulty with some of his lines, and the director was losing patience. "I can't help it," the actor said. "It's those damn eyes. Every time I have a scene with Rachel, her eyes drive me crazy!" The director told him to stare at her forehead instead.

During the next scene I shared with Rachel, I made a point of looking directly at her. Her eyes reminded me of Nickel's in their ability to suggest an otherworldly power, but the phrase that leapt to mind was Jenny's: devil's eyes. These were not God's eyes, like Nickel's, but they possessed similar power. They dared me to ask her out, they dared me to sleep with her, they dared me to be swallowed up. One night after we had been together, I awoke, gasping, gulping for air. I had dreamed that I had dived into a black pool and plunged down, down, down. My lungs were burning, but I knew I could not surface until I touched bottom. Mercifully, I awoke, having just realized that there *was* no bottom to reach.

I was inexplicably apprehensive with Rachel after that night. Fortunately, the play was staged and ended soon after, and I offered weak but plausible excuses to avoid her. I had now turned my thoughts toward seeing Nickel again.

There was no reasonable justification for the heightened anticipation on which I fed during those weeks prior to the event. I must have known that the ceremony would afford little if any chance to be alone with her; I must have recognized that this was also Mick's graduation, and the two of them would be united by their mutual accomplishment. Yet, each time I unfolded Nickel's letter and reread her simple words I envisioned what it might be like, and each time I embellished this vision slightly more, adding brilliant, vivid strokes, seeing in the letter untold promises, unspoken devotion.

To this day, I think there was an audible crash on that long-hoped-for weekend, when my vision careened into reality.

And I also believe that I was forewarned of this impending collision. On the night before I returned to

Burton for Nickel's graduation, I dreamed again of the blackened pool. This time, however, a woman cloaked in white beckoned me in, assuring me by her calm that the pool was safe, and so I dove headlong, streaming past the white garments, plummeting into darker and darker depths, ultimately colliding with jarring force against a rock-ribbed base. My mouth opened, and I gulped coal-black water.

Thirteen

Since Friday was scheduled as a study day prior to exams, I left early that morning and arrived home at noon, the day before the graduation ceremony was to take place. My own high school graduation seemed much longer ago than three years, but I could recall that week's heightened festivities clearly, and I knew that Mick and Nickel would be undergoing similar rounds of celebrations.

It was an occasion for a stream of parties and dances, not the least of which was the Prom, held on the Saturday prior to graduation. The Prom was an event billed for so long as the pinnacle of one's adolescence that one could scarcely avoid reaching a pitch of fervid excitement as that day dawned.

Girls spent months agonizing over whether anyone would invite them (it was unthinkable to go alone, or "stag" as we said) and months agonizing over their dresses. Despite this excessive tribulation, they all seemed to look remarkably alike when the evening came: the dresses all strapless confections of white, pink or blue; the faces filmed with rouge, eyeliner, and eyeshadow to match the colour of their dresses or the colour of the sashes which inevitably circled their waists;

the hair either piled in sophisticated sleekness atop their heads or painstakingly curled and stiffened with hair spray; their shoes duplicating the hues of their dresses; dainty stoles or sweaters reposing on their shoulders; tiny white evening bags embroidered with pearls or sequins slung over their wrists.

The boys were equally tormented, enduring weeks agonizing over whom to invite to the Prom and extraordinary anguish speculating as to whether or not she would accept. They also spent weeks, possibly months, earning the money to pay for the carefully selected rented tuxedo (whose cummerbund and tie matched the date's dress or sash), the girl's corsage (whose ribbon also matched the dress or sash), the Prom tickets, and enough reserve cash for the after-Prom visits to restaurants and cafés to flaunt the finery and prolong the evening.

My own experience, I am sure, was typical. I had reached such a peak of ebullience by the time I picked up my date that I could only deflate slowly, like a sinking soufflé, as the evening wore on. Throughout the evening, I had the odd sensation of standing outside myself and observing, wondering, "Am I having fun?" and then, "I should be having more fun than this." There was a tremendous sense of time rushing past, leaving me idly in its wake, blinking, stupefied by the commotion. And after it was all over, I, like most of my classmates all over town, crawled into my own bed at four o'clock the next morning, assuring myself, "So! That was a Prom. I have survived. It was incredible fun," knowing instinctively how compulsory it was to believe this, aware that in the days and weeks, perhaps months and years to come, my friends and I would recapture the "enormous" and "outrageous" excitement of that night over and over and over again, so that when we were older we would have this dreamy, enchanted memory to relish.

It has always seemed peculiar to me that the best memories, the clear and lasting and treasured ones, result from the unplanned events in my life. Sadly, the most tragic recollections also derive from unplanned, unforeseen occurrences.

Having indulged in reminiscences of my own Prom as I travelled home that day, I was, by the time I arrived, enormously jealous that Nickel had just waltzed through this week with Mick. They had glittered, no doubt, at their Prom, and I wondered, enviously, whether theirs had been more thrilling.

Jenny was reclining on the couch in our living room when I entered. "I feel wretched," she said, and she did look paler than usual, her lips colourless, her face devoid of make-up. She said that she had felt fine when she arrived, but suddenly "sank like a big stone in a pond". When she said it was probably the flu, I moved to the farthest side of the room. I do not much like throwing up. Our parents had gone to the doctor's, she informed me, for my father's regular check-up.

"What are *you* doing here?" she asked. She lay with one arm covering her eyes, and I was grateful that I did not have to meet her stare.

I hedged at first, saying that I needed a quiet place to study, was eager for some home cooking, and needed to do my laundry. Then I mentioned that, besides, it was graduation weekend.

"So?" she said. "I haven't seen you rushing to these ceremonies the last two years. What's the attraction? Oh! God, Daryl, you're not here because of Nickel, are you?" She removed her arm and turned two rather watery eyes my way.

"Will Mom and Dad be home soon?" I asked.

"You're avoiding the question. God, Daryl." She recovered her eyes. "Probably. So, what's this hang-up you have with Nickel? I thought you'd be over that by now."

"Do you want anything from the kitchen?"

"You have to have an invitation, you know."

"To the *kitchen*?"

"Ha, ha. To the *grad-u-a-tion*. God! Don't tell me the Queen of Sheba *sent* you an invitation?" She propped herself up on her elbows and turned to accuse me. When I did not answer, she said, "Daryl, just tell me one thing. Please. Just tell me what is the big attraction with that girl. What is it that you pathetic boys find so irresistibly compelling? Huh? What is it?"

I entered the kitchen, but this did not deter Jenny. She raised her voice. "She's got that poor Mick nearly out of his mind. He can't take a step without wondering what Nickel will think. She's got her father nearly out of his mind too, hovering over her, wanting to lock her up in a glass cage so no one will touch her. She's got every other damn boy at school drooling and mooning over her whenever she walks by. What is it? She hardly says anything. She just walks along like she owns the goddam world. What is it? I expected more from you, Daryl. I expected you would be above that sort of – of, God, of all that *crap*."

"How's Maple?" I asked, re-entering the room.

"Oh, for chrissake!"

"Want a beer?"

"God, no!" She sat up, shook her hair loose, pinched her cheeks, looked at her watch. "Oh! I've got to go – sorry I can't stay and continue this one-sided conversation. Tell Mom and Dad I'll stop by later. I thought they'd be back by now."

It was not until I saw my parents' astonishment when they discovered me sitting in the kitchen, that I realized

I had forgotten to tell them I was coming. In all my elaborate visions of this weekend, I had not only completely neglected to inform them of my plans, but I suddenly was aware also that I had never responded to Nickel's invitation. It seemed an uncanny, irresponsible oversight. Where could my mind have been?

When I mentioned that I had to run over to the Malleys to let Nickel know I was coming to the ceremony the next day, my parents exchanged a look. "Anything wrong with that?" I asked.

My father shook his head back and forth, back and forth.

"Something wrong?" I repeated.

"It's hard to say, Daryl," my mother said. "Hard to say. That family seems all out of whack lately. There's Imogen always crying her eyes out and she won't say why. If I ask her, she'll say, 'Am I a good mother? Am I a good wife?' Now what can you say to that?"

"Worrier," my father said.

I thought he meant my mother, but she took her cue from him. She could read beyond his one-word sentences.

"All the time. She worries all the time. She thinks Doug is going to go down in one of those planes he's flying in. She thinks Joey is going to flunk out of school. She thinks Danny is on drugs, what with all those weird things he's been painting."

"What about Nickel?"

They exchanged another look. "What *about* Nickel?" my mother said.

"Does Imogen worry about her too?"

"Never even mentions her. The other day I was over there and I asked about Nickel, you know, if she had a good time at the Prom and all, and Dan came up behind Imogen and he sank his fingers into her shoulder. I think he hurt her. She made a face. It was almost as if he was warning her not to talk about Nickel."

"That's ridiculous."

It was then that I made my fateful trip over to the Malleys, and it would be the last time I saw Dan Malley alive.

Fourteen

I walked through the back yards, the route I often took to the Malleys. Ours was a friendly neighbourhood, the boundaries of our yards not delineated by fences, but only by low flowerbeds or bushes. I sometimes wonder how the events of that day might have been altered if I had approached by the road and entered the front door. There I might have been safely sequestered, perhaps chatting with Imogen or Nickel, instead of thrust into the middle of the fray outside.

In any case, the garage door was open, and Danny was inside. Before him, on the workbench, was the box which I knew sheltered the revolver. He flinched slightly when I called to him, or perhaps I imagine this in my hazy recollection.

It was warm on this day in late May, and Danny wore a white T-shirt emblazoned with red and black swirls which, he informed me, were his own design. "What is it with red and black?" I asked. "Your favourite colours?"

"Love and death," he said.

I am sure this is what he said. I am convinced I have not fabricated this after the fact.

I heard the back door slam and saw Dan Malley coming down the steps toward us. To his left, at the screened kitchen window, Imogen was peering out at us. I waved at her, but she did not acknowledge my gesture. She was watching Dan.

We exchanged some light banter while Danny removed the gun from the box. "Ever use one of these?" he asked me.

"No."

"Want to try?"

"Here? You don't shoot it here, do you?"

Both Danny and his father laughed, and I felt foolish. Dan said that they practised at the firing range. "Want to join us?" he asked.

"What, now?"

"Sure, we could go now."

"Well," I lied, "I have to get back. I only came over to tell Nickel I could come to graduation tomorrow."

"Oh?" he said.

"That's OK, isn't it?"

Dan shrugged. "Suit yourself."

Danny was rubbing the revolver with a soft cloth. "Here," he said, "I'll show you how to load it. You can come with us another time."

I started to protest, but Danny was going to load it anyway, I could tell. He opened a box of bullets, showed me how to load the gun, then emptied it, and handed it to me. I did not even like holding it, but I feigned interest. It was surprisingly warm from Danny's touch, the handle ribbed, the barrel gleaming. Although it was heavier than I had imagined, it still looked and felt remarkably like some of the toy guns we had played with as children. It was easy to load.

Mick's car pulled in the driveway, and I thought I heard another car pull up in the front of the house and a door slam, but from where I was standing, I could not see that car. Mick and Nickel stood for a moment in the driveway, whispering and glancing covertly in our direction. They turned and walked around the front of the house. In a moment, I saw Imogen again peer out the kitchen window, and I could see Mick and Nickel behind her. Their voices reached us only as low murmurs. I thought then that I saw someone else in the kitchen, but I could only see a white shirt. Perhaps it was Joey. I laid the gun on the bench.

"Is Joey home then?" I asked.

"No, doesn't get home until the end of June."

From this moment on, things begin to blur in my recollection, but I think that we then heard loud voices from the kitchen, and a woman's shout. We stood there, absurdly regarding the house, all of us, I think, straining to listen. Abruptly, the back door opened and Mick stormed down the steps, his long arms and legs propelling him forward, his shock of black hair reminding me of the omnipotent Prospero. He looked pained and stung, but also angry.

Nickel's face joined her mother's at the window.

Stupidly, oafishly, I began to back away from Dan and Danny as Mick approached. It was obvious that Mick was preparing himself for a confrontation. I was embarrassed, thought it none of my business. I had intended to go into the house to see Nickel, but as I saw her and her mother peering out the window, I sensed that I would not be welcome there either. Still, I was not prepared to leave the scene entirely. I stepped slowly around the side of the garage, thinking, I suppose, that I would give them a few minutes and then wander back. I stood at the back of the garage, I'm not sure for how long, perhaps only a few minutes. I remember staring at a white sheet flapping on the clothesline and at the newly dug section of Imogen's flower garden. I could hear angry voices – Mick's and then Dan's.

I continued around the garage, stopping to stare once again at Danny's "Apocalypse Two" mural. I heard Mick say, "She's pregnant!"

Rounding the corner, I saw Dan backed against the workbench, Danny off to one side, and Mick facing Dan, fists clenching at his sides. Mick said, "Did you hear me?"

Dan looked stunned. Both Danny and I moved toward them.

Dan said, "What the hell—" and put his hand down on the workbench.

One would think that horrific moments such as those which followed would be indelibly etched in one's memory. This was not the case with me, nor was it the case with Imogen or Nickel. A blueish gauze filtered down over that afternoon, only to be occasionally lifted by the sporadic breezes of capricious recollection. What happened next I have only pieced together over time, from these snatches of revelations and from what others have said, although what they have said varies considerably. I could, later that day, remember the shot and a very low sort of growl emerging from Dan and the look in his eyes, briefly, a wide, dazed gaze. My police statement offers other odd details: a peculiar, oily smell, dark, sticky blood, Nickel's scream, an awful, horrible wail from Imogen, and the sight of Jenny kneeling over Dan, her long hair brushing against his bloodied shirt.

There were an ambulance, police, crowds of people. I remember sitting on the back steps, gaping at that sheet flapping in the wind.

82

Fifteen

Dan Malley was not dead when the ambulance removed him that day. He was unconscious, and we all knew he was seriously injured, but I do not think any of us believed he could die. After sitting, stupefied, for an hour, maybe two, on the Malleys' back steps, wagging my head back and forth, inanely repeating, "It was an accident," to anyone who approached, I apparently was taken to the police station along with Mick and Danny. There we tendered preliminary statements. I was unable to read Mick's or Danny's, but mine, I know, was virtually incoherent, as I have suggested. The police would later take a second statement from me, but quite early on it was evident that the shooting would be ruled an accident. Although it may have been merely small-town courtesy, for we knew these policemen, their wives and their children, none of us were ever treated as potential murderers. Our examiners were deferential, sensitive to our mutual grief and shock.

In any case, I remember little about that visit to the police station and have only a vague recollection of the drive home with my parents. They settled me in my room after some discussion about whether or not they should summon the doctor. A dull, thick feeling had invaded, as if there were layers and layers of cotton stuffing between me and the outside world.

It must not have been until the following day that lucidity began to return, for the next clear moment I remember is when I heard that Dan Malley was dead. I was sitting in the chair beside my bedroom window, when my father entered. It was surprising that he had brought the news, for it was unlike him to tackle this sort of mission.

"Dan Malley—" he said, and I went cold from the mere mention of the name. "Dan Malley—" He began again, stopped, lifted Nickel's picture off my dresser, stared at it, replaced it. "Dead," he said. "Sorry." He put his hand on my shoulder briefly, stood there awkwardly patting me, and then left. In my right hand was an odd sensation, a tingling, as if I had squeezed something rough or ridged. I would have been unable to remember when I had last cried, but I did that day, like a child, with enormous sobs, until I lurched for the bathroom and vomited up quantities of dark, watery fluid.

Those next few weeks were survived through meticulous concentration on the most minute details. At school, I studied voraciously for my exams, imbibing the most trivial details. Between feasts of studying, I devoured superficial details of my daily routine. I would think: I am taking a shower. The water is tepid. I am washing my neck, my left shoulder, my right shoulder. I am combing my hair. It is too long. I need a haircut. On and on like that I went, staying afloat on this driftwood of minutiae, fearing that if I gave my mind its freedom, it would spill me into a swampy morass wherein I would sink.

In the three days I had remained at home before returning to school, few people attempted to discuss the incident with me, except for their vain attempts directly following the shooting. Sensing that I was teetering on the edge of enormous grief, and that I needed time and solitude to grapple with that sorrow, they left me alone. My parents engaged in a fair amount of whispering during that time, but I was not capable of curiosity yet. They could have spoken in normal tones, and I still would not have heard. I had only inquired about Nickel once, and my mother had said that she was "taking it hard". A few weeks later I learned that she had not spoken to anyone since her father was shot.

After my last exam, I returned to my dormitory and began systematically packing my belongings. I carefully boxed items for summer storage and carted these crates, one by one, across campus to the storage facility. I meticulously packed two suitcases, completed all the requisite departure forms, conveyed what I am sure were rather insubstantial and distant goodbyes to my friends, and boarded the bus which would return me to Burton and to those chapters which I would begin to tear through, as my comforting driftwood began its slow deterioration.

"Nothing will ever be the same," my mother said.

"Damn right," my father added.

We were sitting in the back yard beneath the apple tree, my suitcases lying where I had dropped them by the back steps. A swarm of gnats hovered inches in front of my face. I brushed at them absently, wishing I could postpone this conversation until I was able to regain my bearings.

"Joey vanished. Nobody knows where he is. And Doug, why, he only got a five-day leave and now he's gone too. Imogen – do you know about Imogen?"

I did not, so she informed me. Imogen was in a convalescent home, still suffering from shock.

"Bonkers," my father said.

"Well, not exactly bonkers," my mother corrected. "She's in shock, dear."

"Crazy as a loon."

"Barney!"

"Anyway, Claire's over there now—"

"Claire?"

"You know, Imogen's sister, from Detroit, the one with the fake eyelashes. You know the one?"

"Oh."

"She's over there trying to cope with all that mess. Phone calls and people still dropping by with chocolate cakes and tangerine-marshmallow salad and everybody wanting to know how Imogen is and what happened to Joey and how is Danny Jr taking it and has Nickel talked yet."

"What do you mean?"

"Well, Nickel hasn't said a word. Not a word since Dan," my mother paused to touch her fingertips to her forehead, "rest in peace–since Dan was—" Her head bobbed helplessly from my father to me and back again. "Everybody, I mean *everybody* has tried to get Nickel to talk, but she remains hidden up there in her room, like a little mouse. Danny carries her breakfast and her lunch and her dinner up there every single day, but she hardly eats enough to keep a bird alive, Claire said. You want anything to eat, Daryl?"

I declined.

"And Mick. Well. Did I send you the articles?"

She had, but I had pointedly and wilfully not read them, which she sensed immediately.

"You didn't read them? Daryl, what's got into you?"

"Sorrow," my father said.

"Oh my, Daryl, I'm sorry, of course I know how you must feel. Jenny is all torn up too—"

My father stood and went into the house.

"—just all torn to pieces."

"Jenny?" I said.

"Seeing something like that, especially when—"

"Jenny was there?"

"Why, Daryl honey, you are just all shot to bits. Of course, she was there. Why, you know she was there."

I must have known this, of course. It was included in my police statement; I could recall seeing her bending over Dan, the ends of her hair tinged with blood. Still, there was something askew in this portrait, and although I could not have said what this was, it bothered me.

"These gnats are annoying," I said. "I think I'll go unpack."

In my room, I once again retreated. "The sweaters go in the middle drawer. The blue sweater. The grey sweater. The socks go in the top drawer." The decision whether to hang the shirts in the closet or to place them, folded, into a drawer, and if so, which drawer, suddenly took on monumental significance. Incapable of making this decision, I became increasingly agitated, scuttling from the dresser to the closet and back again, like a frightened animal trapped in a cage. When I caught sight of myself in the mirror, I was both appalled and disgusted, and I sank into the nearest chair.

I forced myself to think about Nickel. I began by reconstructing that day, from the moment I left my house to cross the back yards, but in my recollection, I foundered, impeded by minute details which compelled me to backtrack, begin again, each time adding cumbersome trivia. Over and over I left the house, I crossed the Taylors' back yard, I stepped over some flowers. No. I descended the back steps, I crossed our driveway, I stepped over our hedge, I walked across the Taylors' lawn, I stepped over Mrs Taylor's geraniums, I stepped into the Foleys' back yard. No. I descended the back steps, I circumvented the garbage can, I crossed our driveway, I stepped over the peony bushes and stooped to examine a brilliant monarch butterfly. No.

It was as if I were unable to repeat that journey. I dreaded disembarking at the point where everything had gone awry, where fatal steps were taken, where I would not be able to retrace and alter the events. I abandoned the effort and escaped into sleep.

When I awoke, I was irritable, unnerved. I had been dreaming, but could not immediately recall the dream. Then, as I looked across the room, spying Nickel's picture on the dresser, I heard the words, "She's pregnant."

The familiar nausea returned, and I was propelled back into my dream. I sat bolt upright. Nickel was pregnant. Veiled and loathsome questions had been lurking on the fringes of my memory all these weeks, questions which I had been unwilling to dislodge. At that moment, however, they began to spill out, unbidden.

Rounding the corner of the garage that day, after hearing Mick's words, I had looked into Dan Malley's face, and I had thought, instinctively, that Dan was being accused of this violation, that Dan had fathered a child by his own daughter, that Dan had abused her, that Dan had committed the unspeakable. At the time, I could not have said exactly why I was so convinced of his guilt. It was as much the look on Dan's own face, I am sure, as Mick's demeanour. Mick was not apologetic. He was outraged, his stance accusatory.

Now, however, in the dim light of my room, I wondered if I had erroneously leaped to that conclusion. Surely it was more logical that Mick had fathered Nickel's unborn child. Why did I not automatically suspect him?

The most sickening thought of all was: why was Dan Malley dead and not Mick MacNeil?

By the time my mother announced that dinner was ready, I had crumpled a dozen sheets of paper and had begun again. "I came down the back steps," I wrote, sweating profusely, writing feverishly.

"My God, Daryl," she said, "you're *sick*!"

I must have presented an appalling sight as I turned toward her, for she retreated to the door. "I'm calling Dr Feeter!" she said.

"No! You're *not* calling Dr Feeter."

My tone frightened her, and she took two more steps backward, calling, "Barney!"

"It's all right," I said, regaining control. "It's all right. I just need to think a while." I knew, then, that I was compelled to see Nickel, and though I dreaded it, I was also oddly elated at the prospect.

Sixteen

On my way to the Malleys, Mrs Taylor hailed me from her house. Behind her screened door, she leered at me, and although I wanted to pretend I had not heard her, she repeated her summons. "Daryl. Daryl Wilson!" I turned. "Come here, if you please."

I stood on her porch as she remained secure behind her barricade. In her black dress with starched white collar, she resembled a modernized Puritan.

"Well?" she asked.

"Pardon?"

"Well, how *are* you, Daryl? How are you taking it? Isn't this horrible?" She leaned forward, peering up and down the street, her forehead pressing lightly against the screen. Glancing behind her, she whispered, "A person's almost afraid to leave the house."

"Mm."

"I keep this door locked." She tapped at the inside handle, confirming that it was indeed locked.

"Mm."

"Don't you think someone should be in *jail*?" she said. "I mean I know all you boys said it was an accident. I mean I know *you* wouldn't be a murderer. But, really, *someone* had to pull the trigger, right? *Someone* had to do it. But *someone* hasn't said he did it, right?"

"Mm."

"Was it Mick? Was it Danny? Who was it? Why isn't someone in *jail*? At least someone should be in jail temporarily, don't you think? Daryl?"

"Mrs Taylor, I—"

"Who did it? You can tell me. Mick says it was all his fault, I know. I read the papers. But he didn't actually say he pulled the trigger, now did he?"

"It was an accident."

She clucked her tongue, pressed her lips together. "Why won't Nickel talk? Why won't anyone say who pulled the trigger? A person's afraid to go to sleep at night. I knew that girl was too good to be true—"

"What girl?"

"Why, Nickel. Nickel Malley. I knew there would be trouble sooner or later."

"Goodbye, Mrs Taylor—"

"But Daryl! Wait! Daryl, who did it? Daryl?"

As I knocked at the Malleys' red door, it occurred to me that I might encounter Danny, with whom I had not spoken since just before Dan Malley was shot. I very nearly turned and fled at the prospect of seeing him, but just then Imogen's sister, Claire, opened the door. She looked very like Imogen, with the same drawn, tight look about her face but without the characteristically red-rimmed eyes. Instead, her eyes were outlined in black, the lids pasted over with heavy, black false eyelashes. Claire seemed older than Imogen, her dark hair spun through with grey, her stocky figure draped in a matronly blue smock. She hesitated before letting me in, but recalled my name, if not my face.

When I asked for Nickel, she looked puzzled. "She won't see anyone," she said. "Didn't you know that?"

"I thought I might try—"

"She's locked in her room. She won't talk to a soul."

The phone rang. I heard Claire say, "No, nothing. We're all set. No, she hasn't. No, no change in Imogen either. No, no word from Joey." She seemed to expect each question, to have heard them all before, many times. "Yes, I will. I surely will. Thank you very much." As she turned, I knew that she anticipated a similar barrage of questions from me, and although I wanted to ask them, I refrained. It took some manoeuvring, but I finally prevailed on her to let me attempt to speak with Nickel.

I tapped at her door. "Nickel? It's Daryl. Nickel?" All was silent, eerie almost. I knocked several times, pausing to listen between knocks. No sound of breathing, no sound of movement, no sound at all could be heard except a dog barking somewhere down the street. Through the keyhole, only a desk and a chair piled with clothes were visible.

In the kitchen again, I said, "How do you know she's OK? How do you know she's even in there?"

Claire leaned forward suddenly, smashing a fly against the table top with a fly-swatter and scooping up the remains with a napkin. "This has been going on for weeks," she said. "I'm not going to break down the door. She eats what Danny takes up there. He leaves the tray by the door and she waits until no one is around and then she takes the tray and eats some of the food. Then she puts what's left back outside the door. But she won't talk. She comes out to go to the bathroom. I've seen her. She looks OK, surprisingly." Claire had rehearsed this speech, it seemed, and had delivered it to others. "The doctor came once. He said to let her be. He said it will take some time and that as long as she is eating and isn't violent, we should just wait and see. Look out," she said, as she swung the fly-swatter against the side of my chair.

The front door slammed and I stood.

"It's only Danny, I expect," she said.

I was at the back door in an instant. "Sorry, didn't realize—" I blurted, or something equally inane, feigning intense interest in my watch, hurrying out the back door, unaccountably terrified at seeing Danny again. But once outside, the garage loomed before me. Half expecting to see a huge red stain on the driveway and the same sheet flapping on the clothesline and Dan Malley lying there on the ground, I bolted across the back yards until I was safely in my own house once again. Some hero, I thought.

Jenny and Maple were nestled beside each other on the couch in the living room. My father huddled in his chair, tossing popcorn out the window. Jenny looked uncharacteristically timid, leaning into Maple, her arms wrapped about her protectively. One of Maple's massive arms draped Jenny's shoulder, and the other cradled a beer can against his rounded belly.

"Hey there, Daryl," Maple said. "How you holding up? Huh?"

"OK. Fine."

My mother breezed into the room, saying, "You'll stay for dinner? Oh Daryl, you're back? Where were you? Someone called. Some girl."

"Oh?"

"Linda Loman."

Jenny snorted.

"What's so funny about that?" my mother asked. "Where were you, Daryl?"

Adopting my father's mumble, I managed, "At the Malleys." When Jenny flinched, Maple pulled her against him and began fumbling with strands of her hair.

"Oh?" my mother said. "Did you see Claire? How's Nickel? How's Imogen, did she say? Have they heard from Joey? Was Danny there? Maybe I should send over some meatloaf."

Perched on the edge of the coffee table across from Jenny, I asked her, "Tell me about Mick," but before I could continue, Maple had lumbered to his feet, pushing Jenny roughly aside in the process.

He said, "Damn it, I've heard all I can take about that goddammed Mick and I'm not gonna sit here and listen to any more of it."

My father threw a fistful of popcorn out the window, my mother coughed, Jenny sat up straight. "For God's sake, Maple," she said.

"For God's sake, nothin', I'm sick to death of it."

"Dinner will be ready soon," my mother said. "I'll go see—"

"We're not staying," Maple said.

"Honestly, Maple, you are so rude!" Jenny stood. She was wearing an unflattering baggy purple sweatshirt over skin-tight purple slacks. Letting herself go, I thought, though she still wore a load of bracelets on her arm, which jangled as she waved her hand at her husband. "You have no patience!"

"*I* have no patience? *Me?* For chrissake—"

"Why don't you stay for dinner?" my mother asked.

"Popcorn!" my father demanded.

"Oh, Barney!" My mother retrieved the bowl and walked toward the kitchen, glancing back helplessly as she went.

"You stay then," Maple said. "You stay and talk about that goddammed Mick all you want. I'm going home."

"You do that!"

"I will."

"Go right ahead."

He did, he left, beer can in hand, tyres peeling on the driveway, dust trailing in the wake, a real exit.

"I guess I said the wrong thing," I offered, to no one in particular.

"For God's sake, Daryl!" Jenny burst into tears. My father stared absently out the window, and from the kitchen came the sound and smell of popping corn.

Seventeen

The fourteen-mile drive from Burton to Green Falls is a tranquil one along winding country roads, dipping in and out of gently sloping valleys. After nearly a week at home, floundering aimlessly, performing my daily pilgrimage to the Malley household to rap at Nickel's door, and returning each time more dejected, I undertook this drive to visit the Green Falls Public Library.

For my purposes, I could have walked four blocks from my house to the Burton library, but Burton's librarian was Liza MacNeil, Mick's mother. If I had asked her for newspaper articles about the shooting, I would have encountered queries and probing for which I was not prepared.

On that July day, with its spectacularly clear sky, I passed top-heavy trees, blue-green in their density, and rows and rows, endless rows, of grape vines whose tendrils, like skinny arms spread and tied to wire crosses, stretched to touch their neighbours. It seemed incongruous to me that here, outside of Burton, in these scattered white frame houses perched astride a curve, people might be having breakfast or washing their windows or oiling a bicycle, unaffected by Dan Malley's death.

At one curve, I passed a greying outbuilding with a rusted tin roof. Against the side of the building leaned a curly-headed teenaged girl facing a boy whose arm pressed against the building beside her head. They turned toward me as I passed, proffering gazes of such clarity and innocence that I felt sick. All of that had ended for me. I had drifted on into a sinuous maze, and this clear sky and these aimless curves were merely an enticing entrance to something more foreboding. I had that feeling one gets when driving a familiar route, that the vehicle hastens along of its own accord and that one is propelled forward, unable either to stop or turn back, precipitated toward the incontrovertible end.

There was a time when I was younger that I had been obsessed with watching clouds. I wondered where the first "piece" of cloud was formed and whether, if it had begun elsewhere, the cloud would look different? I was intrigued by all the forces that were constantly changing the shape of these billowy masses. If Mrs Taylor watered her geraniums, would that added moisture, evaporated into the atmosphere, generate a cloud? And what if she did *not* water her geraniums? Would that speculative cloud not exist? It seemed to me that so much in the world was initiated by chance, but that once initiated, various forces conspired and collided to propel one along a road such as this, like those clouds which were hurled through the sky.

*

The Green Falls librarian, a slim woman with bright red curls, said, "From last *month*? You want issues of the *Burton Herald* from last month?"

"Yes."

She gazed steadily, as if she were offering me a chance to reconsider. Finally, she said, "Well, OK. They're downstairs. Marge—" Calling to a woman shelving books in the New Fiction display, she said, "Marge, over here – got a dungeon request for you." She handed Marge the slip of paper on which I had written the dates of the issues.

Marge eyed the request suspiciously. "They'll be dusty," she said, shrugging her shoulders and leaving the room.

Waiting at a secluded table, I watched the red-haired librarian stamp books. From a stack at her left, she carefully removed the top book, placed it in front of her, and opened it to the middle. Then, turning the pages tenderly and moving her lips as she eyed each number, she found the page she sought, held the book open with her left hand, reached for the stamp with her right, gently rolled the stamp on the ink pad, and lovingly stamped the page. She leaned forward to inspect the imprint. Then she took a sheet of paper from a pile directly in front of her and placed the paper over the fresh ink, patting it briefly, and cautiously closed the book. She placed this newly stamped book to her right and retrieved another volume from the pile at her left.

With a start, I realized that I was doing it again, escaping through intent focus on precise, rather meaningless tasks.

Marge returned with the newspapers which she dumped unceremoniously on the librarian's desk. The red-headed librarian gave Marge a reproachful glance, smoothed the papers, and brought them to me, placing them reverently before me.

"Whatchew want these for?"

"Oh. Writing a book," I lied.

"A book! Really? On what?"

"Well—"

"Is it *secret*? Oh geez, is it *secret*?"

I nodded.

"Ohhh. My. Ohhh." Reluctantly, she returned to her desk.

On the day after the shooting, the *Burton Herald*'s headline was: LOCAL MAN SLAIN!! Beneath the headline was a blurred picture of an ambulance with part of a stretcher hanging out the back. Dan Malley's feet, splayed awkwardly, were just visible. Beside the ambulance stood Imogen Malley, face to the camera, wide-eyed, as if the camera itself were a gun. On the far left was a huddled figure with hands to her face, Nickel.

The article said that Dan Malley had been "gunned down in his own back yard at three o'clock in the afternoon, broad daylight". He had come home from work and "an argument ensued with a local boy, Henry ["Mick"] MacNeil, aged 18, son of Carl and Liza Kay MacNeil of 419 Carver Avenue". According to the article, "Dan Malley was shot by young MacNeil apparently as he tried to wrest the gun from the boy's hand. Mr Malley died at 7 p.m. at Burton County Hospital. The MacNeil boy and two other youths present at the shooting are being held for questioning."

Held for questioning? Is that what it was?

The rest of the article noted that Dan worked at Poly Automotive, that his "survivors" included his wife Imogen and four children: Douglas, Joseph, Nicole and Dan Jr, that Mick attended Burton High, that Mick's father, Carl MacNeil, owned Mac's Cadillac, that his mother, Liza Kay, was Burton Public Library's librarian, and that Mick had two brothers, Rockwell and John. Nowhere was my name mentioned.

The article ended with three quotes from "unidentified local residents". The first said, "My guess is that Mick [Henry MacNeil] was going to shoot Nickel [Nicole Malley]. He loved that girl, but you know how fickle girls is. Dan probably just got shot trying to protect his own daughter, that's all. It's a shame."

The second resident said, "Wouldn't surprise me none if the girl didn't shoot her own father – you know family squabbles – and the boy took the blame."

And the article closed with a quote from a third person, "That girl [Nicole Malley] is different."

The headline of the next day's *Herald* was "MURDER OR ACCIDENT???" Beneath it were three pictures: one of Dan Malley, one of Nickel, and one of Mick. Mick's and Nickel's pictures were formal high school graduation poses. Dan's looked like a family snapshot; he stood beside a tree, smiling.

This article said that Mick and two other youths, the "deceased's son, Daniel Malley Jr, aged 16, and Daryl Wilson, aged 21", had made statements, saying that "it was all an accident". Mr Malley was shot while he was trying to show the youths how to use the gun.

The reporter said that Mr Malley's wife, Imogen, and his daughter, Nickel, both of whom were home at the time of the accident, were not available to confirm the statement. Mrs Malley had been taken to Burton Memorial Hospital, "suffering from shock". Nickel was "not available for comment".

A "friend of the family, neighbour Mrs Wilma Taylor" was quoted as saying, "Accident, my eye. They was arguing. I heard them. And there was more people there. I don't know who." Police, the reporter said, "are investigating this allegation".

On page three of the same issue was an editorial titled: "HOW SAFE ARE WE?" In it, the paper's editor asserted that "until the police get to the bottom of this – and let us hope they can do what we are paying them to do – that boy (killer??) better stay in jail."

The next day's headline read: "TRAGEDY OF BURTON FAMILY CONTINUES UNSOLVED". The lead article reported that neither his wife nor his daughter were present at Dan Malley's burial. Only his sons, his brothers and sisters, friends, and "scores of townspeople" attended. His wife was still suffering from "extreme shock" in Burton Memorial, and his daughter was "in seclusion".

The red-headed librarian tapped me on the shoulder, and I covered the headline with my arm.

"You find what you're lookin' for?" she asked.

"Oh. Well, no, not yet—"

"You reading about them murders?"

"Murders?"

"That one over in Burton? By that kid?"

"Oh. No. Rather, yes. I did notice—"

"I know his momma—"

"What?"

"That kid who murdered that man – I know his momma, Liza MacNeil."

Oh God, I thought.

"We was at a conference together just last week. I met her there. I didn't know she was the murderer's mother right away—"

"He isn't a murderer—"

"Oh?" she asked.

"It says here that it was an accident."

"You believe everything you read in the papers?" The librarian's glance suggested I was a fool. "They let that kid out of jail after no time at all. Accident! Ha! I don't believe it for a minute."

"Uh?"

"That Liza Kay, his mother, is a real nice lady. And you know what she told me?"

"That her son was a murderer?"

"No! Of course not. You can't expect a mother to say that. But I knew he was, just by the way she didn't want to talk about it and all. Someone told me who she was and I asked her if she was the mother of that boy who killed the man in Burton – that's the way I put it – I didn't say 'murderer', but she didn't want to talk about it. Of course she didn't, if he was guilty, don't you think? But she did tell me, when we got to talking the next day after our seminar, she told me her husband had a heart attack. That was right after all this mess. I felt sorry for that poor woman. To have a son who's a murderer and then to have your husband have a heart attack. He didn't die though."

"The father?"

The librarian nodded. "Well, we're closin' in thirty minutes. You done yet?"

"No. But I'll bring these up to the desk when I leave."

"We close in thirty minutes."

"Yes, I know."

"Will you be done then?"

"Yes, I'll be done then."

"OK, then. You bring those papers up to me when you're finished. I sure hope you find what you're looking for."

I had time to read one more article: "GUNMAN RELEASED!!!" Beneath it was a picture of Mick, the same graduation picture that had appeared in the previous article. This article reported that Mick had been released from jail, that he hadn't actually been in jail anyway, being a minor, not yet eighteen years old. This corrected an earlier version that said he was eighteen. The article said that charges were not being pressed, that Dan Malley's death had been ruled an accident. It reported that Mick was staying with "an uncle in an unspecified location". It also reported that Mrs Malley was still in the hospital and that the daughter, Nickel, remained "in seclusion".

The article quoted a local teacher who "happened to witness the shooting". To my surprise, this teacher was my sister Jenny. "According to Mrs Branch's statement," it said, "the shooting was an accident."

I had not been aware that Jenny had made this statement, that she claimed to be a witness of the shooting, or perhaps I had merely buried this knowledge along with other things I could not face.

A few days later, when I returned from yet another futile trip to the Malleys to tap at Nickel's door, I found Jenny sitting in our back yard watching my mother weed around the peonies. I asked Jenny about her comment reported in the newspaper. My mother glanced around at us, saying, "Oh, Daryl."

Jenny said, "I'm not going to talk about this."

"*Did* you witness the shooting?" I asked.

"For God's sake," she said, "I wasn't *actually* a witness."

"You weren't *actually* a witness? What does that mean? How could you say you were? How could you tell the police and the reporters—?"

"Daryl, will you just listen? I know that boy. I know Mick better than his own mother knows him. He wouldn't kill anybody."

I thought this an odd thing for her to say. I wondered if, then, she thought that I or Danny were more likely to kill someone. I wondered if she had actually seen the shooting.

Our mother said, "Well, he'd kill a damn bumble-bee—"

"What," I asked, "were you doing there anyway? *Where* were you?"

"Some lemonade anyone? Iced tea?" My mother had abandoned the weeding.

"Daryl, for God's sake! What's the matter with you, anyway?" Jenny looked both puzzled and frightened. "*You* were there. Why are you torturing me about this? Don't you think I feel bad enough?" And she commenced a flood of tears, over which my mother clucked and soothed.

"Daryl, let her be. This has been too hard on her."

"On *her*? Jesus. What the hell's going on around here anyway?"

"Daryl, now watch your language."

"Christ."

"Daryl! I didn't send you up to that university so you could learn how to swear. You remind me of that Cannibal in your play."

"Cannibal? You mean Caliban?"

"Whatever. The one who said his only profit from learning language was that he knew how to curse."

Jenny was sobbing more audibly, and if I had not seen her cry so often for so little reason, I might have been more sympathetic.

"Just let it be," my mother said. "It's over and done, so let it be. Don't go turning back those pages—"

"Right," I said, but I was now more convinced than ever that I had missed some vital pages.

Eighteen

Although I had given little thought to summer employment, I was offered a position at the realty company for which my father used to work. Mr Slocum, the owner, had visited my father one afternoon and, hearing that I was unemployed, asked if I would be interested in filling in, "doing odd jobs", in his office for the summer.

Most of my peers have either an innate loathing of or an imperious need to step into their parents' shoes. I joined my fellows in the former category, having heard so much real-estate chatter during my youth that I had long ago sworn that this would be the last field I would enter. Despite the deluge of facts about commissions, percentages, markets, contracts and mortgages which my father dropped on our unwilling heads, I had managed to obliterate any comprehension of these concepts. In short, I knew next to nothing about the real estate business. However, lacking the energy to seek an alternative, and, surmising that the position would probably consist of sorting mail and filing papers – just the sort of mindless occupation of which I was in need – I agreed.

I had not anticipated that the other four employees of Slocum Realty would be disappearing for vacations throughout the summer and that rarely would there be more than one or two others shoring up the office. Of these, at least one was always out showing a house, and so I became a virtual answering machine, and like the machine, could only record messages. Rarely did I know the answers to any questions I was asked and often was berated for my ignorance. "Did that house on Grover Street go yet? You don't know? Isn't this Slocum *Realty*? Who *does* know, then?" and "What's the current interest rate? You're not *sure*? Isn't this Slocum Realty?" and

"No one's been by to see my house. Yes, it's listed with you. Why hasn't anyone been by? Is this Slocum Realty or not?'

The humiliation of being unable to answer these queries blasted me out of my lethargy, forcing me to acquire some rudimentary knowledge. Still, the time I most dreaded was when someone would come in to inquire about listing or buying a house. If none of the realtors were in the office, the secretary, Joanie, would turn these people over to me. "Just get their names," she said. "Make them feel like you know what you're doing. Someone else can get back to them."

But people were not satisfied with leaving their names. They asked questions and they wanted answers.

On one particularly grey day, I was staring out at the clouds hanging low over the building facing ours, when Joanie tapped at my door. "Someone to see you," she said.

"What about?"

"Not sure. It's Mrs MacNeil."

"Oh, God."

"Just get the details. Tell her someone will get back to her."

"Oh, God."

When Mrs MacNeil entered, I was struck by her resemblance to Mick: thick, dark hair, black eyes, the same brooding quality to her expression, the same slim physique. It was as if, like a photocopier, she had plunked out a duplicate of herself, in a masculine version. She was simply dressed, in a white blouse and dark skirt, and wore sturdy black pumps at which she was staring.

"Dog poop," she said, twitching her nose.

The odour had reached my nostrils as well.

"Be right back," she said.

104

When she returned, she said, "I like dogs, don't get me wrong, but wouldn't you think people would watch where their animals did their duty?"

"Yes."

"You can't still smell it, can you?"

"No. No, I don't think so."

"Well, then."

"Mrs MacNeil? Is that correct?"

"Yes," she said, extending her hand.

"I'm Daryl Wilson."

She pulled her hand back slightly. "Oh. You work here? I didn't know—"

"Just for the summer."

"Oh. Well." She glanced behind her, at the open office door, as if seeking an alternative to me. She considered me for a moment, sighed, and said, "Well, then. How do we proceed?"

"Proceed?"

"I want to sell."

"Sell?"

She looked behind her once again. "My *house*," she said.

"Ah, yes. Of course. So you and Mr MacNeil want—"

"Not him."

"Not him what?"

"Not him, he doesn't know that I'm going to sell it."

"Will he agree?"

She shrugged. "Doesn't really matter."

"But if it is in his name—"

"It's not. It's in my name. Are you sure you can't smell that dog—?" She peered at her feet. "After his heart attack, we switched everything."

"Oh. But still, he would agree—?"

"Does it matter?"

Actually, I did not know. "Well, I suppose not—"

"Well, then."

"So you want to move?"

"Of course I want to move. That's why I want to sell the house. This *is* Slocum Realty?" she asked, eyeing the walls, peering at a licence hanging on the wall behind me. Although the licence did not bear *my* name, she seemed reassured by it.

It was none of my business, but I asked why she wanted to move, and she responded, "What do you need to know that for?"

"If you want to move because the roof is falling in or the plumbing does not work, we need to know that." I had heard Mr Slocum say this to a client the day before.

She stared at me. "Are you the Daryl Wilson who was at the Malleys when Dan Malley was shot?"

"Pardon?"

"You heard me."

"Yes, then. Yes, I am."

"Then why don't you just tell me about it?"

It was my turn to glance around the office. *Was* this Slocum Realty? Had she been wanting to ask me this all along? Did she have any interest in selling her house?

"I'm sure that Mick has already done that—"

"Mick doesn't talk much. He suffers. He said it was all his fault, but what does that mean? Did my son pull that trigger?"

"It was all an accident—"

"Haven't I heard that before! An accident, oh, I've heard that. But why was Mick's name all over the papers, why won't people look me in the eye, why did he do it, *did* he do it? You were there. Tell me."

"Everything happened so fast—"

"Do you know someone's writing a book about this? Someone's going to call my son a murderer—"

"Who? Who's writing a book?"

"We won't ever get away from it. Yesterday, a lady called me from way over in Green Falls, some lady I met at a librarian workshop. She told me that some man had come in her library and wanted to look at a bunch of newspapers about the murder. The murder! She said this man was going to write a *book* about it."

Oh God, I thought.

"We're not staying around for some nosy man to come prying about my Mick and writing a book saying he was a murderer. We're not staying around for that."

"Maybe she was mistaken. Maybe your friend, this librarian—"

"She's no friend. I just met her once."

"Maybe this person that you just met once – maybe she misunderstood. Maybe this man isn't really writing a book about—"

"Oh, she didn't misunderstand! That's just what he told her. He told her he was writing a book, and then he took out all these Burton papers and started reading all the articles about the shooting."

"Maybe he was reading something else in those papers—"

She looked exasperated. "How do *you* know? This lady told me—"

"OK. OK. She is probably right, then."

"Are you going to tell me or not? I'm willing to believe it was an accident. I believe that. But one of you had to pull that trigger and I just want to know who it was. Was it Mick? Why are you three boys all pretending like that trigger just got pulled by a puff of air?"

"Maybe we don't *know* who pulled it."

"Sure," she said, "sure. Maybe two of you don't, but you can't tell me that the one who actually pulled it – you can't tell me that that one isn't staying awake nights."

I removed my hands from the desk and slid them to my lap, as if she would be able to detect some stigma on my fingers, some telling sign that I had fired that gun.

"Forget it then," she said. "Just tell me how I sell my house."

I explained that I would go through the house with her and take measurements, that someone from the agency would suggest a price, advertise the house, and offer an open house.

"An open house? You mean you're going to let people come in?"

"Yes. People have to see the house—"

"Damn," she said. "Damn. I hate people nosing around."

"I'm sorry, but—"

"OK then. OK. Just do it."

Nineteen

As surprised as I had been to see Mrs MacNeil enter my office, I was even more stunned when Jenny arrived the next day. She breezed in, unannounced, saying, "So? You actually still have a job?"

"You don't look so well," I countered. Her skin was dull and sallow, her eyes enshrouded with dark shadows, but oddly glistening. Sarcastically, she thanked me, and when I asked if something were bothering her, she said, "God, Daryl! You're not *that* insensitive, are you?"

I had thought that I was suffering as much as anyone else, but apparently I did not wear it as visibly.

"Listen," she said. "How much do you know?"

I closed the office door. I had been waiting for this. I explained that apparently I did *not* know quite a lot, but that I did know about Nickel. She seemed puzzled. "I know," I said, "that Nickel is pregnant."

Incredulous, she demanded to know the source of that information. "Mick," I said. It was true that Mick had not actually told *me*, but at the time, I did not think it necessary to make the distinction.

"*What?*"

"Don't look so surprised. Surely, with you and Mick being so close—"

"What the hell is that supposed to mean?"

"I can't believe he wouldn't tell *you* that piece of news."

"And I can't believe he *would* tell you!" she said. "God!" And without a word of explanation, she left.

Two days later, Jenny phoned me at work. "God, Daryl," she said. "Mick's gone."

Mr Letner, a client, was sitting in my office. He was a grizzled, nervous fellow whose fingers tapped a steady beat on the edge of my desk. At the same time, his head regularly punctuated this beat with violent jerking, as if he were endeavouring to throw his skull off his neck. I had been with him for ten or fifteen minutes and my own head was beginning to jerk empathetically. I smiled at Mr Letner as I listened to Jenny, overly conscious of forming my replies into business-like phrases.

"To what destination?" I said, stiffly.

" 'To what *destination*?' Jesus, Daryl, what's the matter with you? He's gone. Gone!"

"And when did this occur?"

"You idiot. You ass. This *occurred* sometime yesterday."

"And the destination—"

"For Godsake, Daryl, if I knew the goddam 'destination' I wouldn't be taking the trouble to worry about it and I wouldn't be taking the trouble to phone you."

I smiled at Mr Letner. "And the reason for the departure?"

"The 'reason for the *departure*'? God! *You*! You're the goddam reason. I told him what you said about Nickel and he said it was a lie. Then he hung up on me! Now he's gone. *You*. You're the reason."

"I?"

"Oh for chrissake," she said and hung up the phone.

"Thank you so much for calling," I said to a blank tone. "I am glad I could help."

Mr Letner's head jolted wildly and my own head followed suit. During the rest of his visit, I had that sensation of standing both within and outside a scene, mouthing words mechanically while simultaneously observing my own ineptitude at a distance. What was Jenny on about anyway? So Mick had gone away. What did that have to do with me?

Two days later Mick MacNeil was dead.

I heard about it at work. Returning from lunch, Joanie told Mr Slocum, "Want to hear something *awful*? The MacNeil kid is dead!" Then, seeing me, she said, "Oh! You *know* him – oh, Daryl! His mother thought he was gone, and then she found him hanging in the basement. Can you imagine how awful—"

The news flapped at the edge of my brain like a tiny, flying insect. I did not believe Joanie. "That's a poor joke," I said. "Sick."

"But it's *true*," she insisted. "It's *true*."

I had been scheduled to visit the MacNeils that very evening to take the statistics of their house. I had a quick vision of me descending the steps to their basement

110

and seeing poor, young Mick MacNeil swinging from a beam. But Jenny interrupted this imaginary discovery as she came tearing into my office, slamming the door behind her.

"God!" she whispered. "Oh God, Daryl, you have done a terrible thing."

"*Me?*"

"Mick is dead."

"I just heard."

"My God, Daryl. Mick didn't know about Nickel."

"That's not true."

Jenny, however, insisted that Mick had called me a liar and had hung up on her and now he was dead. By her reasoning, it was my fault for conveying this "news" about Nickel. It was fitting that Jenny would not consider the impact of her own role as bearer of the news.

I insisted that I had heard about Nickel's pregnancy from Mick. "Although, it's true," I groped, "that he did not actually tell *me* but I was there. He told Dan—"

Like a punctured balloon, Jenny's bravado deflated as she sank into the chair by my desk. "When was that?"

I told her that it was right before Dan was shot and she wanted to know what Mick had actually said, what had been his actual words. "I did not hear it all. I merely heard him say that she was pregnant."

"Nickel? He said, '*Nickel* is pregnant'?"

When she put it that way, there was a small but noticeable shift in my mind, as if the contents of one closet were spilling into an adjoining one. "I think he said, 'She's pregnant.' She. Nickel."

" 'She'? Oh Daryl," she said. "You fool. You complete fool. Nickel isn't pregnant. He wasn't talking about *Nickel*."

But I did not hear whom he *was* talking about just yet, because Mr Slocum entered, saying that I was needed on the phone. Jenny, her face drained of colour, left. Although I wanted to call after her, I could not imagine myself bellowing, in the middle of Slocum Realty, "Who *is* pregnant?" and so I refrained.

Perversely, I did visit the MacNeils to measure their rooms. That I waited until a week after the funeral and phoned first to confirm my visit was neither decorum nor courtesy. It was fear and guilt. I had once again sunk into an empty limbo, retreating from the questions germinating at the back of my mind. I remember thinking that I would have to sit down and evaluate all of this soon – not yet – but soon. Meanwhile, I should merely listen and absorb, like a sheet of blotting paper.

"Suffering," my mother says, "builds character," and she will add, "or at least it *ought* to." What she does not say is that character building is a gradual process. Like a big vessel, it is made slowly.

I could not look out a window in the morning without thinking: Dan Malley won't ever see a morning again. Neither will Mick. I could not turn on the radio without realizing that neither Dan Malley nor Mick would ever hear a song again. Everything reminded me of Dan Malley and Mick MacNeil.

Three days after Mick's death, I returned to work, still relatively worthless, mired in a blue haze in my office. But when I heard Joanie tell Mr Slocum that *someone* had to take the measurements of the MacNeil house, I volunteered. They looked at me queerly.

The local newspapers, of course, had headlined Mick's death: "MOTHER FINDS SON HANGING IN BASEMENT", and later, "SUICIDE NOTE FOUND". Would Mick have realized that his last letter would be summarized for the entire town of Burton to read? I scrutinized these articles, expecting to see my own name, expecting to be identified as one who had "done a terrible thing".

Nickel was not pregnant?

The second article, "SUICIDE NOTE FOUND", quoted one line of Mick's final letter, found on his desk, addressed to Nickel Malley. The quoted line was: "I am sorry for my part in your father's death." The reporter then reminded Burton's readers that Dan Malley's death had been ruled an accident but that "poor young MacNeil was tragically traumatized by his role in this deed".

I do not know what I expected to find at the MacNeils. Some clue to Mick's death? Some explanation for Jenny's saying I had "done a terrible thing"? In one of my imagined scenarios, I saw Mick going to the police before he hanged himself, telling them that it had been I who had fired the gun, and I envisioned the imminent knock on my door or being surrounded by police cars as I drove down the street. I pictured a classic, stark grey cell (in truth, the Burton County Jail's cells were painted green), and I even saw myself sitting forlornly on the edge of a narrow bed, head in hands. The impulse to feel guilty and to give the Furies free rein came naturally to me.

The MacNeils lived in a grey three-storeyed clapboard house on a pleasant street. The house, neatly painted with fresh white trim and decorated with window boxes overflowing with geraniums, fronted a small lawn, its tall, unkempt grass a contrast to the pleasing look of the house. Through an open window at the front, I could hear birds – parakeets? – chirping from within. It did not appear to be a house of grief.

Mrs MacNeil opened the door. She had that slack look that I had seen so often lately in my own mirror, and although it was a warm July day, she wore a dark cardigan which she wrapped more closely about her as I entered.

113

She said nothing. When I said I had come to measure the rooms, knowing that she had been expecting me, she merely looked slowly about her, as if to say, "Here it is; go right ahead." I measured all the rooms on the first floor, and because I was nervous, I noticed very little – a beige carpet, a blue couch, the cage of parakeets.

The basement was dark and clammy, its cement walls and floor giving off a chalky, musty odour. I measured quickly, my eyes riveted to the floor, avoiding the ceiling. Beneath a work bench in the corner was a length of electrical wire; a loop of heavy rope dangled from a hook.

Before I went up to the bedrooms, I asked permission, but Mrs MacNeil only shrugged. Knowing that Mick's two older brothers now lived elsewhere, I was surprised to see the bedrooms as they were. It was as if all three boys were still living at home and had merely stepped out for a moment.

Beyond the master bedroom, in the next room, which I presumed had belonged to the two older brothers, were bunk beds. On each was a folded towel and a sweater thrown casually at the foot. Shoes, a football, a basketball, and a helmet lay in one corner. On the wall were graduation pictures of the two oldest boys, a pennant, a dartboard, and two football posters. The desk was stacked with books, notebooks and letters.

On the door to the third and smallest bedroom was a hand-lettered sign which said "MICK'S ROOM: KEEP OUT!" Inside, the bed was neatly made, but the covers were turned back, as they might be in a hotel. A shirt with rolled-up sleeves hung on an old-fashioned coat rack, and on the chair next to it lay a pair of blue jeans – not folded, but tossed over the back as if they had recently been taken off.

There were books and letters on the desk in this room also. I listened for sounds of Mrs MacNeil and heard her, below, clucking her tongue at the birds. Two framed pictures of Nickel stood at one corner of Mick's desk. In one photograph, Nickel appeared to be about twelve years old. She sat on a fence, smiling sweetly at the camera. An angel of God, I thought, an angel of God. In the other picture, Nickel, in a bathing suit, seemed to have been caught off guard, for she was looking to her right, beckoning to someone off-camera.

Riffling quickly through the letters, I recognized Nickel's handwriting on several and another handwriting that looked familiar, but which I could not immediately place, on several others. Then I thought, what am I *doing*?

I neither read nor took the letters, but I wanted to. Instead, I measured the room.

A few days after visiting the MacNeils, while emptying a drawer in my own room (part of my mindless rituals), I found an old list of grammar exercises. The sentences were written in my own hand, but on the reverse side, Jenny had listed terms and examples. The list was not only a stinging reminder of those days when she used to tutor – and slap – me, but it also, I realized, bore the same handwriting as that on some of the letters in Mick's room.

Never having formed a close relationship with a teacher, I was unable to fathom this intimacy between Mick and Jenny, a familiarity that would allow them to exchange letters. Whether out of jealousy or ignorance, I was suspicious of this relationship, and I gratefully turned my scorn from myself toward someone else.

I readily dredged up charges against Mick and Jenny, thinking how naïve I had been not to "connect" them earlier. A month or so later, just before I was to return to school, I saw Jenny leaving our house as I returned from work. As she got into her car, I said, "Everything OK?"

"No," she said, casting me her best look of contempt, "no thanks to you," and she slammed her door.

Then, in August, as I came down for breakfast one Saturday morning, I heard her talking with my mother in the kitchen.

"Don't you two say hello to each other any more?" my mother asked.

Jenny grumbled; I said hello and then, with my cornflakes in hand, took the seat opposite her. She quickly stood to leave, and I said, "Are you putting on weight?" I had never known her to be swathed in such loose, blousy garments when she could be showing off as much of her figure as possible.

"God, Daryl, you are so dense."

My mother eyed me as if I had just dropped through the roof into her kitchen. "Why, Daryl Wilson, where have you been the last few months?"

Jenny pulled her long shirt tight against her abdomen revealing a distinctive, solid bulge. "I'm *pregnant*, you idiot."

"Why didn't anybody tell me?" I asked.

Jenny, in exasperation, was studying a fixed point on the ceiling. My mother said, "Jenny didn't want anybody to know for a while, but Lord, she's been telling people for a month at least. I'm sure I told you. Didn't I tell you, Daryl?" My gaping stare was answer enough. She turned to Jenny. "Didn't you tell him?" she asked her.

Dumbly, I said, "Does Maple know?" As soon as I said it, I realized the idiocy of the question, and Jenny was quick to highlight this.

"God, Daryl," she said. "You need some help."

After she left, I asked my mother, "When did she get pregnant?"

She had been standing at the sink, her back to me, but at this, my mother slowly turned her head toward me, bestowing on me that stare that I had often seen in Slocum Realty, the one that usually preceded the question "This *is* Slocum Realty, isn't it?" She said, "What an odd thing to say, Daryl. People usually ask, 'When is she *due*?' not 'When did she get pregnant?' She's *due* around Christmas. As for when she got pregnant, I don't know, you'll have to figure it out yourself." But then she began to figure aloud, holding her fingers aloft as she counted backward. "Let's see: December, November, October, July – no, August—" She began again. "Wait. It must have been March. 'Cause that's the third month and nine and three make twelve. March."

The only thing I could remember about March was that I had appeared as Prince Ferdinand in *The Tempest* that month.

That night I dreamed of Jenny and Mick. They were appearing in a play very like *The Tempest*, but they kept changing roles and I was the director, yelling at them to learn their lines, learn their lines. Jenny recited Miranda's lines and I screamed at her that she was not Miranda, and Mick was trying to be Ferdinand, but I insisted that someone else had that role. What remained with me throughout that next day was the connection of Jenny and Mick, the connection of them as potential lovers, and this was enough to give my mind something to feed on. I resurrected all sorts of "evidence" to support these growing insinuations: Jenny's endless "tutoring" of Mick, even when he was no longer her student; Maple's jealousy; Jenny's letters on Mick's desk; Jenny's concern with his "departure" and her horror over his suicide. All sorts of evidence.

Twenty

Oddly, in that year after Dan's death, when I was nearly stupefied with grief and confusion, I was able to accomplish what I had, in my comparatively more lucid years, been unable to bring to fruition, and that was winning the hand of Nickel Malley. It was, to say the least, a bizarre courtship.

I had continued to visit the Malleys nearly every day during that summer, to knock at Nickel's door. Imogen's sister Claire was still in residence, acting as a veritable field marshal. She would bolt through the house propelling the vacuum or brandishing a dust cloth or flapping a fly-swatter. Tempting concoctions were always simmering away in the kitchen, filling the house with their savoury smells. Yet, aside from her own bustling activity and its attendant hums, flumps and thuds, the house remained quiescent. I did not encounter Danny, nor did I enquire as to his whereabouts. Imogen was still convalescing away from home. When I asked about Imogen, Claire would say, "Oh she's very strange, very strange. It will take her some time. She's got everything mixed up – her childhood, her early marriage – and leaps from one to the other as quick as that." Claire snapped her fingers in front of my nose.

Claire had heard, finally, from Joey, who was with a friend in Kentucky. "He's growing tobacco," she said. "Communing with nature." Nickel remained in her room.

One Saturday, about two months after Dan died, on a day indistinguishable from any other on which I had visited the Malley household, there was a faint noise from Nickel's room as I tapped at her door. Since I had always been greeted with complete silence, even the slightest sound from within was remarkable. I had even begun to imagine that she no longer existed, spinning fantasies that she was away somewhere and I was foolishly tapping at the door of an empty room. But when I heard this noise – did she say "Come in?" or did she say my name? – I turned the doorknob, and was stunned to find the door unlocked.

Blue and white curtains hung at the windows, casting an eerie bluish light through the room, over a green stuffed chair, a small vanity table, pale blue carpeting, and a bed covered with a white quilt decorated with a red and green apple design. Only Nickel's dark hair and the side of her face were visible beneath the quilt.

I had not anticipated that she might appear changed, for there was an image of Nickel which I retained in my mind, and in this vignette she was always tanned and radiant, her skin luminous, her dark hair shining. She looked very small there in that bed and her face very white, like the face of a porcelain doll. Against that white skin, her eyes, when she turned them toward me, were prodigious and haunting.

Not knowing what else to do, not thinking really, I climbed into bed beside Nickel and pulled her toward me, much as I had done years ago in the tent, when the world had seemed full of promises. We lay there for some time, not speaking, with my arms around her and her own arms curled against her chest. I searched for

119

something to say, a way to begin, and just as we grasp at clichés in moments like these, I pulled someone else's words out of the air.

It will sound foolish now, but I began reciting Ferdinand's lines from *The Tempest*, bits and pieces of what I could remember, much as one might sing a lullaby to a frightened child. I went on about how I would "rather crack my sinews, break my back, than you should such dishonour undergo", and "'tis fresh morning with me when you are by at night", and "Admir'd Miranda! . . . worth what's dearest to the world!" Imagine.

People in love do nauseatingly sick things. Some speak baby talk, some dream up impossibly inane nicknames, I recite Shakespeare. The first words that I heard Nickel say since before her father was killed were on that afternoon when she said, "Do you love me?" It was whispered, I knew it was Miranda's line, and I was surprised that Nickel knew it, but I was programmed to that cue and declared, "O heaven! O earth!" In my mind, I could hear Jenny's snorting, derisive laughter, but it did not matter. I went babbling on, rushing toward my line which would cue her to say, "My husband then?" but when I came to it, she missed the cue. She did not know the play *that* well, I reasoned, and in fact she did not say anything else that day.

The next day, I returned with a copy of the play and I again climbed into bed beside her and began reading aloud. I recited only Ferdinand's and Miranda's parts, and on this day again, she said, "Do you love me?" I responded with my now-fervent line, "O heaven! O earth!" Still, she said nothing more.

We went on like this for a week, although I rather feared that Claire would enter and misinterpret these odd scenes. And finally, one day, after Nickel repeated her one line and I offered my heaven and earth response, she began to cry, gently at first and then more forcibly, expelling boulders of grief.

After that, she was no longer in her room when I arrived. She would be waiting downstairs or on the front steps. We went for walks, she began to talk – though never about her father or Mick or any of the horrors surrounding their deaths.

She was obviously not pregnant. Even if I had not heard this from Jenny, it would have been apparent nonetheless from Nickel's slim frame. She had lost as much weight as Jenny had gained in these past few months.

Too soon it was September and I had to return to school for my final year. I thought seriously of dropping out, of eking out an existence at Slocum Realty, just to be near Nickel, but Nickel was stunned when I suggested it and insisted I return to school. When I asked what she was going to do, she said, "There are a million things on this earth a person could learn to do and not enough days in anyone's life to try them all." That may have reminded her of Dan's and Mick's shortened days, for she stopped then, looking about her as if she were straining to catch the remnants of a fading tune. A month later, after I had returned to school, Nickel wrote to say that she had enrolled in art classes at a nearby college.

We wrote long letters several times a week throughout my last year of school, and I returned home monthly to see her. People were beginning to notice, to talk, but most seemed to approve. They seemed to think that Nickel deserved something "good" in her life and they were under the impression that I was that something good.

Nickel never once mentioned her father or Mick to me during that year after their deaths. Ours was an unspoken pact that allowed us to talk of anything and everything else, but when the conversation veered dangerously toward mention of either Dan or Mick, one of us would raise a new subject, rescuing us both from what we knew was dangerous and forbidden water. And so, for that time, we were lulled into a false sense that the past can be effaced with a quick sweep of the mind, that the present and the future could fill all the spaces of the past.

I did see Danny finally, before I left for school that September, and then again several times on my visits home. But we were never alone, and we talked awkwardly, exchanging the banter of strangers straining to be polite. Sometimes, though, he wore what seemed a sly grin, a slight raising of one side of his mouth, and he would nod his head as if in complicity with my thoughts or as if he were aware that I carried an unconfessed guilt, the details of which only he knew.

By the time I left for school at the end of that summer, Jenny was visibly pregnant, in her fifth month, with the baby expected in late December. It was odd to see Jenny and Maple together now. Moving from one misconception to another, I had reasoned that since Jenny was pregnant, not Nickel, then it was Jenny about whom Mick was speaking that day. Why he should have been angry, why he would declare his anger and announce his own adultery to Dan Malley were questions I could not answer. Although I was already painfully aware that I had missed most of that crucial conversation, I had created such a lurid vision of Mick and Jenny in my mind by this time and was so relieved to discover that Nickel was not involved that it was easy to ascribe these notions to Jenny and Mick.

Maple and Jenny seemed a changed couple now. He was protective of her, overly so, watching her, staring at her belly, gazing at her face. He was quieter, more soft-spoken, as if he were treading lightly, unsure of his ground. Jenny, too, had ceased her constant fidgeting and wriggling. She no longer wore the clanging bracelets, her skin had taken on a permanent, soft flush, and she seemed more deferential to Maple. She was, however, primarily occupied with her pregnancy and could give you the exact size and developmental stages of the foetus at any time. "Right now, the baby's two inches long," she would say, holding up her fingers and indicating the length, "just about the size of a worm", or "its little brain is forming right now – when do you think it starts to work?"

I might have found this more enthralling if I had not been so preoccupied with Maple's reaction. It seemed insensitive of Jenny to prattle on about this baby so much in front of Maple, given that it was not his child – and of this I was convinced. Could he really not know this? If he did know, he was reconciled to it. In fact, he seemed genuinely interested, even proud, although a bit bewildered like other men I have known, as they witness this miraculous transformation, as they are made increasingly aware that this is an experience they can never wholly comprehend.

On my way home one weekend in November, I had thought I would have to endure yet more talk from my mother about the impending arrival of Jenny's baby. It seemed obvious that my mother had no inkling of the Mick and Jenny saga, no suspicions that the baby was not Maple's. I had heard about the bassinet, the crib, the new wallpaper, the infant layette, even the diapers. Each time I came home, this baby frenzy increased, and as I travelled home that weekend, I was already devising excuses to keep me absent from the house as much as possible.

However, the town was buzzing that weekend with news about someone else. Everyone, it seemed, was talking about Imogen.

Twenty-One

Is there a curious symmetry in the world or is it merely that some of us who need order impose it artificially on a random universe? Just as there had been two deaths that year, there were to be two births, and just as my mother has always said "Birth and death come in threes", so would there be another of each in the not too distant future. My mother believed that the souls of the dead would reconstitute themselves in the next infant born to someone close to the dead. It seemed clear to me which infant inhaled Dan's soul and which Mick's.

For not only was Jenny's baby about to enter the world, but so was Imogen's. Imogen had returned home that third week in November, very pregnant indeed. I was greeted with this news shortly after I arrived. "Isn't it *wonderful*?" my mother said. She thought this baby would be "just the thing to restore Imogen". It was "marvellous" that Imogen would have "another piece of Dan" to remind her of him. At the time I wondered what my mother would have thought if she knew that her own daughter soon would deliver a piece of Mick MacNeil.

Nickel had not mentioned her mother's pregnancy to me, even though she had visited Imogen while she was "convalescing" and therefore had to know. All that Nickel had said of those visits was that her mother was "coming along", but that she "gets things mixed up sometimes".

But while my mother seemed deliriously happy for Imogen, filled with enough joy over Jenny's baby to spill over to her neighbour, Jenny was clearly mortified at the news. "I wish you'd quit going on about Imogen," she said to my mother. "I wish you'd just stop!" And when Jenny had left the room, my mother whispered, "She's touchy now, it's natural." From the other room, Jenny shouted, "I am *not*!"

Through all this, my father sat in the living room, in his chair, clipping photographs from *National Geographic*. A stack of pictures lay on the end table, and on the floor were piled twenty or thirty mutilated magazines.

Jenny had eased herself onto the couch, her hands supporting her abdomen. "I feel like a beached whale," she said. "God." She strained to look out the window. "God, I can't even move any more. Where *is* that Maple?"

I started to ask when Imogen's baby was due, but Jenny interrupted me as soon as I mentioned Imogen's name. "Don't you start, Daryl. I can't take it if *you're* going to start."

My father ripped a page out of a magazine and held it up. "Armadillos," he said.

"Jesus," said Jenny.

I knew she was frustrated with her bulk, but she looked beautiful to me, more so than when she was her pre-pregnant trim self.

"Quit staring at me," she said.

*

125

I phoned Nickel, suggesting that she meet me somewhere, but she did not want to leave her mother alone. "Just come here," she said.

"But won't it upset her?"

"Why would seeing you upset her?"

Was Nickel that naïve? "I thought she might associate me with – or blame me for—"

"Daryl, she hardly knows where she is. She hardly knows who *I* am."

"Why didn't you tell me she was going to have a baby?" I suppose I should have waited until I saw Nickel in person to ask this. There was a long silence.

Finally, she said, "We'll be here all afternoon. Come when you can."

So. We were going to pretend that her "very strange" and no doubt very large mother was in no way altered from the Imogen I had always known.

And pretend we did. As Nickel and I sat at the dining-room table, Imogen floated through the house, drifting from room to room. Unlike Jenny, Imogen seemed not at all impaired by the added weight. She wore an expressionless mask, a vacant stare, as she glided in and out of the room, like a mad Ophelia. Several times I flinched when I thought she would surely bump into the table or a cabinet, but she always managed to veer clear. She spoke, but not to us. Once she said something about "little Joey in the sand box, peeing his pants", and another time it sounded as if she were reciting a grocery list: "lettuce, onions, tomatoes, do we have any mustard, pork chops. . ." But the most disturbing thing she said was, "Don't hit me, don't you dare hit me." She was standing beside the table addressing me.

"I would not do that, Mrs Malley."

Nickel looked up when her mother spoke and stared after her as she left the room, but she would not meet my gaze.

"When is she due?" I asked.

"Any day, I think."

"Any *day*?" I asked why she had come home now, why she had not remained in the convalescent home to give birth to her baby. Nickel did not know. I asked what Imogen would do. "Can she take care of a baby?"

Nickel shrugged. "I can, I suppose."

"*You?*" I had an image of losing Nickel again – not, this time, to another man – but to a wailing infant.

Imogen's daughter was born two days after I returned to school. Nickel phoned me, excited, breathless. "She's magnificent!" Nickel said. She was also, for the time being, nameless.

And my sister Jenny's daughter pushed her way into this world three weeks later, just two days before Christmas. I was home for the holidays, and my parents were beside themselves, delirious – or my mother was, at least. My father seemed rather calm until we visited the hospital and saw the dark-headed infant. After that, his face wore a permanent flush. This, I thought, came from his new status as grandfather. Maple seemed proud and awed by his daughter Andrea and entirely befuddled by Jenny's absence.

Maple was in and out of our house while Jenny and Andrea were in the hospital. "I cleaned out the garage and I washed the kitchen floor. What else should I do?" he asked my mother. "What should I get ready?"

My mother told him that Jenny had had everything ready for weeks, that Maple should just relax and enjoy the quiet while he could.

"But shouldn't I be *doing* something?" He was pacing around the table. "I think I'll go paint the living room."

Imogen had still not named her baby. "She doesn't quite seem to understand," Nickel said, cradling the infant in her arms. The child was wrapped in a soft white blanket and when I pulled the cloth back from the side of her face, I was suddenly reminded of a long-ago conversation. I remembered my mother talking about the infant Nickel and her beautiful skin, and of Dan saying that when he touched Nickel's cheek his fingers looked wrinkled and old and yellow, and he thought his life was over. It gave me a chill. This baby frightened me.

And because I was frightened, I asked Nickel if she would marry me.

"Daryl!" she said. "What a thing to ask right now!"

Twenty-Two

Nickel and I were married the following July. I had received my degree in June and had blanketed various privileged companies with my résumé. I had thought: I will be married soon, I will have a job, all will be right with the world. If this simple optimism occurred within a novel, I would readily seek the flashes of lightning, the low drum beat, or any of the tell-tale signposts which clearly indicate impending trouble.

This is how I see "God" or whatever Other Presence there might be – like a careful reader, one who shakes his head forlornly from time to time as his characters plough along rather blindly, naïvely, convinced that if only they think all is well, it will be. I imagine this God occasionally pointing his finger at a tell-tale sign, willing the character to press his head against the warnings and open his eyes. Then, when the fool moves on regardless, this God will either turn aside with mild disgust or lean forward, intrigued by what will happen to this unknowing, naïve figure.

My father died in February, before my marriage. I was at school when my mother phoned to say he had had a stroke. In the hospital he lay mute in his bed, paralysed on one side and unable to speak. His eyes, pools of hazel liquid, roamed over my face and the walls with equal measure. My mother sat at his side, with an odd, silly grin on her face, as if she could make him instantly well by pretending that this was but a minor aberration, a little mistake that would soon be cleared up.

He died the next morning and I was plagued by the notion that although I spoke to him, he may not have heard. Part of my penance was to imagine the infinite things he might have thought when I spoke to him and to imagine the infinite things he might have said to me could he have spoken.

I moved mechanically through the funeral. Throughout the service, I thought of my father and my own grief, and I knew then a measure of what the Malleys and the Mac-Neils had been through. How I would have liked to *open graves and wake their sleepers*.

After the service, I overheard Wilma Taylor say, "The men are dropping like flies. Scares me half to death. If my Roy goes, I don't know what I'll do." She approached Nickel, who was holding her sister, and said, "Let me see Imogen's daughter. Oh my, oh my. Isn't it nice to have something of Dan—" but Nickel turned away abruptly, saying that the baby needed changing.

"I suppose Nickel will have one of her own soon," Mrs Taylor said, her eyes opening widely, staring up at me. "I hope she thinks of a better name for her own, though."

Imogen had refused to name the baby and so Nickel had chosen Penelope. I admit that I had not much liked the sound of it when Nickel first told me. She said that she had first come upon the name when she had read *The Odyssey*, and had therefore associated it with faithfulness, in the manner of Odysseus' wife. "I appreciate faithfulness," Nickel said, but quickly added, "besides, for a nickname we could call her Penny. Get it? Nickel and Penny?"

Jenny was openly derisive, declaring that since she had met Maple, she had been particularly sensitive to humorous or clever names. She mentioned one of her grade-school friends who had been given only an initial, "T", for his Christian name. His surname was Pott. In college, she had known an Ivah Burden and a Winna Lottery and claimed to have read of a man named Jonah Whale.

But Penelope Malley it was. Imogen did not so much ignore the baby as seem puzzled by her. If Nickel would hand Penelope to her, Imogen would take the child, stare down at her, and invariably look back at Nickel as if asking, "Who *is* this?" Once, when my mother visited and cradled the infant in her arms, Imogen said, "It's not Nickel." My mother said, "Of course not!"

Claire had stayed on for a few weeks after Penelope was born, but when she left, the care of the infant lay, as I had expected, in Nickel's hands. Nickel was intrigued by the child, mesmerized by her. On one of my visits, she pressed the baby upon me. Imogen entered the room and said, "Don't hit me."

I was becoming familiar with this. "I would not do that, Mrs Malley."

Imogen peered at the baby. "It's not Nickel," she said.

I agreed.

"Is it yours?" she asked.

"No, Mrs Malley."

"Don't hit it," she said.

On the eve of my marriage to Nickel, I received three pieces of advice. The first, from Jenny, was, "Drag her down off that pedestal." My mother's advice and Danny's advice fell on the other bank of the river, so to speak. My mother said, "Treat her like she's holy, Daryl. There aren't many Nickel Malleys in this world." And Danny had pulled me aside to say, rather cryptically, "Be very gentle. She doesn't know as much as you think." Thinking that he was referring to sexual inexperience, I elbowed him in what seemed an appropriate locker-room gesture, as if to say, "Don't worry, I have everything under control." Danny released an audible sigh and turned away, murmuring something about "rough roads ahead".

The truth is that I was terrified. I can recall standing at the altar waiting for Nickel to materialize at the far end of the church. I was extremely anxious, convinced that she would not arrive. People were smiling benevolently on me, increasing my terror, for I thought at that moment that I was a charlatan, a deceiver, that I had skilfully played some enormous, elaborate trick to ensnare the innocent virgin who was about to be led to slaughter.

And then, as Nickel appeared in the entranceway, her arm through Danny's, the guests gave a collective gasp. No woman, I am convinced, has ever been as beautiful, as calm, as serene, as perfect as Nickel Malley in her long white gown. I wanted to weep. I cannot do this, I thought. I am a Caliban. The minister will surely

131

recognize this inappropriate union, he will surely refuse, he will surely bring scorn upon my head.

But as soon as Nickel's hand was placed in mine and she looked up at me, and those bits of clear white light reflected off her eyes, I thought that someone had blessed me, that I would be altered for the better by what was to come. I could be, I thought, as perfect as she.

How many times had I heard my mother say, "Nobody's perfect"? Hundreds, thousands of times, probably. But nonetheless I thought Nickel was the exception. Her perfection derived from her way of taking life, her way of seeing the world, her ability to accept everyone as he is, to focus only on that "good" portion within each of us. She did not seem to know spite or jealousy or pettiness. And since I knew them all, I was all the more aware that she had little knowledge of them. Was this, I wondered, to what Danny had referred?

After having fantasized innumerable times about our future days and evenings of lustful bliss, when the time came, I could barely touch her. We spent an odd three days at a hotel in Erie, Pennsylvania for our honeymoon. In bed that first night, all I could do was hold her. Something prevented me from crossing the Rubicon. Nickel said, "Well, we're both tired," and fell asleep. When, on the second evening, it became apparent that I was not going to take the initiative, Nickel said, "Is there something I should be doing?" On the third evening, she said, "Do you think I'm going to break or something?" I told her I was not sure, perhaps that was it. "Well, I won't," she said, "although I could get awful dusty just sitting on the shelf."

Back in Burton, I moved into the Malleys' house. We knew that Imogen could not yet stay on her own and that Penelope needed full-time care. I dreaded living there, in the shadow of Dan Malley and in the presence of Imogen, whose mind trailed through labyrinthine passages. Danny was now living with a friend, in an apartment near the university, but he came and went from his parents' house and eyed me with bemusement.

About a week after my marriage, during one of my frequent escapes to my parents' house – or rather my mother's house now – Jenny stopped by with seven-month-old Andrea on her hip.

"How's life with the Queen of Sheba?" she asked.

"How did I ever win her?" I said.

"*Win* her? Daryl, she's not a goddam prize!"

"How will I ever keep her?"

"*Keep* her? She's not a goddam animal either!" She propped Andrea in a high chair, facing me. The child's brown, flyaway hair, gave her an elfish look.

"She's beautiful, don't you think?" Jenny asked.

"Doesn't look a bit like you."

"Ha, ha."

"Nor Maple," I ventured.

Jenny tilted her head cockily. "Oh? And what is that supposed to mean?"

"Looks more like Mick," I said, launching the attack.

"*Mick?* What in the hell is that supposed to suggest?" When I did not answer, she said, "You're sick, Daryl. You're really sick. He was my *student*, for chrissake."

"You're not going to sit there and tell me this is really Maple's daughter, are you?"

"Well, it sure as hell isn't Mick's," she said, yanking Andrea rather roughly from the chair. Over Andrea's wails, Jenny said, "Tell Mom I'll be back later. Tell her I didn't want to sit around here listening to a goddam idiot."

*

133

One Saturday, a month or two later, Nickel and I both visited my mother. She was baby-sitting for Andrea, who was once again propped in the high chair. My mother was making popcorn. "Eat this," she said absently to me. "I can't get out of the habit of making it, and I never did like popcorn." Andrea's large dark eyes fastened on us warily. Nickel, who had not seen much of Andrea, was clearly taken with her and began playing with the baby, singing a rhyme, cooing at her.

My mother asked if I would help her "lug something" in her bedroom. Upstairs, she pointed to a large wardrobe which she wanted moved to the opposite wall. The room was just as it had been when my father was alive. Their bed, with its green coverlet, was situated prominently in the centre, flanked by matching mahogany night tables, each with its own reading lamp. A small green and white striped chair perched in one corner next to a long, low, chest. On this chest were family pictures, the most prominent being my parents' wedding picture. This pair seemed strangers to me, their faces unlined, their eyes bright, their hair glossy. On another wall was the tall wardrobe which was to be moved, and next to it was the closet, its doors flung open.

My father's clothes hung neatly, just as they had always hung: a dozen shirts, neatly ironed; six or seven pairs of trousers; four or five sports coats; one dark and one light suit. On the floor, carefully lined up, were his shoes.

Noticing my stare, my mother said, "I just want to keep them. I'm used to them. They smell like Barney." She closed the closet doors.

We heard the front door open and Imogen call "Sairy?" I was surprised, because Nickel and I had left Imogen with Penelope, hoping that if we began to leave her with the baby for longer and longer periods of time, that she would gradually accept her. For a moment,

I thought she might have forgotten Penelope, but then I heard Penelope's familiar laughter.

Downstairs, Nickel had gathered up Penelope in her arms. Imogen stood stiffly staring at Andrea. "Who is it?" she asked.

"Why, Imogen, that's my granddaughter. That's Jenny's little girl."

It had not occurred to me that Imogen had not yet seen Andrea. She fingered the child's hair. When she saw me, she said, "Don't hit her."

My mother said, "Why, Imogen! Daryl wouldn't do that!"

Nickel was looking at the two babies. "It's uncanny," she said, "how much alike they look."

"Anybody hungry?" my mother asked.

Twenty-Three

Later, after Nickel had accompanied her mother and Penelope home and after Jenny had retrieved Andrea, I, who had remained behind under the pretence of repairing a clogged kitchen sink, repeated Nickel's comment about the babies. "It's uncanny, don't you think, how alike Penelope and Andrea look? Is it because all babies look alike?"

My mother said, "They don't all look alike. Barney's tools are down there." She waved toward a cupboard. "What are you nosing around about, Daryl? You have to keep turning those pages. You can't—"

"—turn them back."

"What's done is done."

"Then it isn't Maple's daughter?"

"Nobody's perfect," she said. And then, "Whose did you think it was?"

"Mick's."

My mother sipped at the air. "It wasn't Mick." She looked around the room absently, and I expected her to offer me something to eat, to find some way to change the subject, but she seemed to make a decision suddenly. She nodded her head. "Jenny was awfully jealous of Nickel," she said. "She's not a bad person, Jenny, just – what is the word I want—"

"Greedy?"

"Oh no, she is not greedy, I didn't mean greedy. More like, ah, needing attention. She needs attention. Don't you think?"

I supposed that was accurate.

"And like I said, she was awfully jealous of Nickel. So, I guess she thought that if she and Dan—"

So. It was Dan and Jenny all along. I was not even very shocked, for the minute she mentioned Dan's name, the chaos began to reveal a distinctive, albeit bizarre, order. I should have suspected it long before. What did surprise me was that my mother knew, apparently with some certainty, apparently for some time.

"Now, Daryl, there's no sense turning back those pages. They made a mistake, those two, and no one could feel worse about it than Jenny, so don't you go stirring up the waters. Everybody has to get on with their lives."

Later, she said, "You can't tell your kids what to do. You just pray to God they won't be too stupid." She gave me one of her knowing glances. "Jenny has a strange way of thinking. She told me it was all Nickel's fault."

"You're right," I said. "It's a strange way of thinking."

"Maybe, now that Jenny has her own daughter, some sense will get beaten into her head. Don't you go telling a soul, Daryl. There's Maple to think about and Andrea too. Don't you go messing with any of this. I'm only telling you so you will shut the book on what's too late to fix. And I mean it."

It was Danny who filled in some of the remaining passages from those old pages. Shortly after my mother's revelation, Danny arrived at the Malleys' house with a can of paint and began repainting the side of the garage, the wall which now bore but a faded rendition of "Apocalypse Two". "Let's get rid of it," he said. "Ready?" He handed me a brush. "Shall we make a clean sweep of it?"

I thought he meant the wall. "Sure."

"It *was* an accident, wasn't it?" he asked.

"I hope so."

"I think about it every day."

"So do I."

"I was only trying to get the gun from Mick—" Danny said.

"*You* were? Wasn't I—"

Danny gave a rueful laugh. "So that's why you've avoided me like the plague? *You* didn't shoot anyone. You didn't get your hand in there fast enough."

I had only a moment's glorious relief, before Danny then asked, "Do you mean to tell me that you married my sister thinking that you had killed our father?"

Ah. Another person might have said this with malice, but Danny, like Nickel, refrains from judgements. It was merely a question, but one which, I now realize, I had been studiously avoiding. What might Danny have thought if he knew that I married his sister believing,

137

also, that I might have been culpable in Mick's death as well?

I will never regret marrying Nickel, but I regret marrying her *when* I did, for it was probably the most dishonest deed I have ever done. But, I had to "have" her, and at some level I must have been convinced that if she would marry me, then I must be free of guilt, for surely Nickel Malley would know the difference between a "Caliban" and a "Ferdinand".

I did not answer Danny's question, nor did he press me further. Instead, he said, as if reading my mind, "Maybe Nickel *knew* that you might have shot him. Maybe she thinks you rescued her." When I still did not answer, he said, "Well. You can't expect a person to be perfect."

"Yes," I said. "Yes, you can *expect* it." I might just as well have opened my shirt to reveal something written over my heart – for all the surprise registered in Danny's expression.

"Then you'll always be disappointed," he said.

If you did not expect it, I thought, what would you settle for in yourself and in others? I had always thought it a glorious and noble pursuit, to expect "perfection", which, in my mind was synonymous with beauty of spirit, nobility.

Danny, reading my silence, offered, "But then, maybe we all have our own ideas of what perfection is. Maybe I call it something else."

Later, as Danny painted over the cloaked figure on the garage wall, he said, "Don't you think it's amazing that Nickel could have that much power? That she could cause so much destruction?"

"Nickel?" I said. "*Nickel* didn't cause any destruction."

"The only reason Mick was out there being the white knight for Jenny was because he was so blinded by

138

Nickel. He was so convinced that if my father could sleep with Jenny and beat his own wife—"

I had wondered if Dan had mistreated Imogen and I had wondered if Danny knew about Jenny, but he dismissed these references with a wave of his hand, as if, of course, they were common knowledge.

"—then my father might as easily move on to Nickel next. And my father was just as determined to keep Mick away from his precious daughter Nickel."

"Why do *you* think your father bought that gun?"

"Who knows? Who knows what was in his mind? To tell you the truth, if he ever *had* touched Nickel, I would not have hesitated to use it on myself – intentionally. Father or no."

That was the only time I have ever seen Danny cry. I stood by, nodding my head inanely. I remember trying to resurrect something I had studied in a Physics class. While I stood there, awkwardly patting Danny's shoulder, it came to me. I could see myself sitting in that Physics class, staring out the window at massive dark clouds scudding toward the building. The professor had said, "Mr Wilson? Something intriguing out there?" As he followed my gaze out the window, he explained the Butterfly Effect. He said, "You may not find this very scientific, but there is a theory that even the smallest movement of an insect – a butterfly, for example – here in this little town could begin a series of reactions that could result in a storm next month in Australia." I had been mesmerized by the idea. Of course, I thought, of course. As I stood there with Danny, recalling this professor's comments, I suddenly wondered if the birth of Nickel Malley – maybe even the conception – was like the flutter of a butterfly's wing. Could her every move have caused enormous consequences? Violence? It was a sobering thought.

But now, as I have had time to leaf back through all these pages, I think that Nickel could only have precipitated all this "destruction" because we placed her in the centre of it. This "big vessel", swirling with misunderstandings and jealousy, was made slowly, by many hands. Mick, Danny, Dan and I – among others – heaped on her layer upon layer of attributes that we wanted to believe existed in this world. It may be true that none of this would have happened if Nickel had not been born, but we can not blame the butterfly for the storm.

I was finally able to sleep with Nickel that night, to "know her" in the Biblical sense. And although this was not quite the perfect experience that I had envisioned – for it was not easy to make love to an angel of God – I would swear that as I burst forth inside her, spilling more than mere seed, I could hear the delicate swish of fragile wings.

Twenty-Four

Does chaos wear the guise of order or is it the other way around?

Nickel is expecting our child in a month. This, then, is the third birth in which my mother so firmly believed. It will be my father's soul the child will take, of course, and my mother was quick to point this out. My father's soul has had to wait a little while, she said, but "Barney always was patient."

Imogen still floats through the house, occasionally admonishing me to please not hit her, and still regarding

Penelope with a vague air of suspicion, but at least Imogen has begun to take care of the child. In fact, there are more promising signs of Imogen's recovery. Recently, she has begun to worry again: "Is that baby warm enough? Is she eating enough?"

Nickel has developed toxaemia. It is not uncommon, but it can be life-threatening, a fact of which I am all too aware. Wilma Taylor accosted me yesterday and said, "I read about a woman just the other day who swelled all up and burst her ankles and died. They saved the baby though and the baby was born with big fat ankles, all puffed up just like the mother." Nickel is in the hospital for these remaining weeks but, as ever, she is Nickel: calm, composed, free of fruitless worry and convinced that no harm will come to the baby.

Nickel is the only person I know who believes so indomitably in the present and, because of that, in the future. I may have rendered Nickel naïve, but perhaps that is because I wanted to believe in a Miranda, however out of step that makes her with my fallible world.

In our bedroom hangs one of Nickel's paintings. I have always been struck dumb by her work. Like Danny, she favours strong, bold colours: bright blues, clear whites, deep reds, bright yellows. There is a pristine quality to the forms. The painting in our room is of a large blue apple, outlined in black and topped with a deep red leaf. A clear white halo surrounds this apple, and floating down the sides of the canvas are bright reddish brown leaves, also outlined in black. It reminds me of Georgia O'Keefe's works, with their pure, entrancing forms and colours. I am jealous of Nickel's paintings because I do not know where they come from. I do not know her mind – only what I have projected into it.

Sometimes it occurs to me that if I did not believe so intensely in the perfection of Nickel Malley, then I might be better able to forgive the imperfections of Dan Malley, of Jenny, of myself and others. The notion of perfection may be as delicate as a butterfly's wing – and as potentially powerful – but those qualities are what constitute its allure.

One might think, now that life seems so ripe with promise, that one could relax, and drink it all in. But it is really at this point, when all is well, that I am most aware of the fragility of human happiness. I am aware of what there is to lose. Nickel is more ready to look ahead than I. I would like for us to hover a little longer here, where it is momentarily safe, but I suppose we have to turn the page.